TONE DEATH

SCHOOL OF HARD ROCKS
BOOK 3

CHRISTY BARRITT

I CRINGED as the unbearable sound of someone chewing entirely too loudly filled my eardrums.

The crunches and slurps were almost too much for me to handle.

But I pulled myself together and did my best to remain composed.

"Camryn, I have to ask: is this what it sounds like for you all the time?" Jinky Jennings, a friend and former college classmate, stood beside me as we stared into the studio on the other side of the glass.

I nodded. "I don't have a normal to compare it with, but I'd say yes."

On the other side of the glass window, Annie King—Jinky's niece—indulged in a piece of crunchy fried chicken, creamy mashed potatoes, and crisp coleslaw. Five high-intensity microphones recorded every mushy slurp and greasy crunch.

Three cameras were set up in front of her, catching every angle on film. Later, Annie would load the videos to the internet so people could enjoy watching her eat.

"This is called ASMR—Autonomous Sensory Meridian Response," Jinky explained. "It's where some people get a physical sensation of euphoria with certain noises, images, and smells. In Annie's case, she focuses on sounds. A certain segment of the population experiences pleasantly triggered responses to the sound of other people eating."

That was seriously beyond my realm of understanding.

I crossed my arms and turned to Jinky. "Your niece actually makes a living at this?"

"A *very* good living." Jinky raised her eyebrows as if she knew exactly how good a living. "She monetized her channel last year, and now does this full time."

"That's . . . amazing." I tried not to listen as Annie slurped gravy from atop the mashed potatoes. The wet, repugnant sound echoed through the speakers of the control room.

It was horrible.

I had audio sensory compulsions—I'd been born

with them. Perfect pitch hearing. Hyperacusis. A complex echoic memory. Those terms all sounded complicated but, to put it in simple terms, most people liked to say that hearing was my superpower.

My perfect pitch abilities had landed me a music contract in my younger years. But, if I wasn't careful, my abilities could become a burden that overran my life until I could barely operate. Lots of therapy throughout the years had helped me hone my skills so they wouldn't be a hindrance.

"This is certainly . . . fascinating," I continued as I watched Annie.

She was in her early twenties and surprisingly thin considering everything she was eating. Her stark, unnaturally black hair was long but pulled into a tight ponytail on top of her head. Her makeup was almost jarring, and her expression was intense.

"She originally wanted to be a singer, but the poor girl is tone deaf," Jinky frowned. "I hated to be the one to tell her. But she was making videos and posting them and . . . they weren't good."

"She prides herself on ASMR with a Southern twist." Lavern Blackmore stepped into the room from the hallway where she'd been preparing the food.

She was Annie's assistant—a tall, thin woman with short red hair. She was in charge of production, as well as switching out the food for Annie.

"Southern twist?" I asked.

"That's right." Lavern nodded, her eyes still on Annie. "Instead of eating the typical Asian foods usually shown in videos, Annie eats a fusion of Southern and Asian. She adds Old Bay to her ramen, makes sweet tea with boba, adds collard greens seasoned with squid. She's done amazing with it."

"It's quite the way to make a living."

"Not to be confused with mukbang, although the two are similar," Lavern continued as she double-checked a camera angle on her phone.

"Mukbang?" I wasn't sure I'd heard her correctly.

"The term basically covers all the food channels you see online. Some people cook. Others have eating contests. It's very popular right now."

Annie finished her chicken then motioned to Lavern, who scurried into the studio to bring Annie some ramen.

As she did, I glanced at Jinky.

I still wasn't sure why Jinky had asked me to come here and listen to Annie. Annie had rented this studio space here in Savannah, and she wasn't associated with the music school where the rest of us worked.

"So . . . I'm sure you're wondering why I asked you here," Jinky started, as if reading my mind.

"I am curious."

"Annie has been getting some threats lately, and I'm worried about her."

A-ha! I knew there had to be more to this.

I glanced at Jinky as she stood there wearing her bright blue kimono and a matching headband around her oversized blonde hair.

She was larger than life in so many ways—someone a person could truly never forget.

Between the lines on her forehead and her down-turned lips, she looked very concerned right now.

"What kind of threats?" I asked.

"At first, they were just text messages." Jinky glanced at her niece as Annie took a bite of a fried chicken leg. "She films multiple episodes in one sitting to get the most bang for her buck—or should I say *muk*-bang for her buck?" She let out a cackling laugh. "Get it? Muk-bang?"

"Clever."

I studied Annie again, noticing that she was slowing down some, that her skin looked paler.

She must be getting full. Not many people could eat six different meals in one setting without puking.

Jinky quickly sobered and her gaze clouded. "Lately, the threats turned more serious, more *deadly*, I should say. Annie started receiving notes. Some were slipped under her door. One note was left inside her apartment."

"Inside?" That was *definitely* more serious. "What did the notes say?"

"I can show them to you later, but basically the person has been sending clever word plays like 'I'm chomping at the bit to see your show end,' and 'Please, bite off more than you can chew,' and 'You're going to regret being tone death'—yes, death, not deaf."

"That's got to be unsettling, to say the least." I glanced back through the glass and watched as Annie grabbed something from a cooler to reset the scene. She seemed to be growing even more pale.

Lavern brought out a fresh bowl of loaded ramen and had touched up Annie's makeup before scrambling from the room.

"At first, she didn't take the threats too seriously," Jinky said. "It's become the norm online, you know? Trolls who have nothing better to do than to be keyboard warriors who hide behind their computers as they hurl insults. Annie figured someone managed to get her cell phone number and was messing with her. But finding that note in her home made her rethink things."

"I can imagine."

Jinky turned toward me. "That's why I asked you to come here. I thought you might be able to help."

"Did she contact the police?"

"No, Annie didn't want to bring them into it. She's not a fan, especially after her brother went to jail for breaking and entering. The police back in Texas didn't handle the case correctly, and it's made Annie skittish ever since. I told her she should, but she refused. When I told her I'd talk to you instead, she really liked that idea."

I let out a deep sigh as I contemplated her words. "I know it might seem as if I'm capable of finding the culprit since I solved a couple of crimes, but—"

"You *are* capable." Jinky locked gazes with me. "I've seen it with my own eyes. You have a natural talent and when you combine that with everything you learned from Phil and even your father . . ."

Phil was my husband, who'd died almost three years ago. He'd owned a security firm. And my father had been a professional con artist, so I supposed I'd learned from both sides of the crime spectrum.

I might be well-rounded, but I wasn't a professional investigator. Not by any means. In fact, I was a former singer turned housewife turned crisis management expert.

"I fear it's just a matter of time until something happens to her." Jinky's voice cracked. "I couldn't bear it if it did. You know how close we are. Annie's like a daughter to me."

I glanced back at Annie, and all my other thoughts faded when I saw her open the top on a covered bowl and pull something out.

A live octopus wriggled in her hand.

She was about to eat it.

I tried not to make a face, but I failed.

It seemed cruel and inhumane and . . . gross.

Almost like an accident I couldn't look away from, I watched as Annie raised the octopus—a fairly small one—and attempted to suck a slimy arm into her mouth, almost acting as if the appendage were a spaghetti noodle.

But as soon as she tried, the creature seemed to sense danger and spread its tentacles. Arms suctioned onto each of Annie's cheeks. Another to her chin. One arm went wild, wriggling around as if searching for an escape route.

Instead, Annie stuffed the flailing arm into her mouth.

I cringed at each slurp. Each rubbery chew. Each time saliva squished in her mouth . . . it was all like chaos to my ears.

I couldn't believe what I was seeing. But I *really* couldn't believe what I was hearing.

I glanced at Lavern. Even she had to look away.

"Does Annie know what she's doing?" I asked.

"Couldn't one of those suctions stick to her throat and choke her?"

"She does all her research," Lavern said. "There's a lot going on behind the scenes. All this is planned out ahead of time."

At once, Annie froze.

Stopped chewing.

A gurgling sound filled the room.

Annie's palms hit the table, and she stood, leaning over. The octopus clung to her face.

She took one hand from the table and tried to pull the creature off.

Then she glanced up, panic in her gaze.

A gagging sound filled the room.

I sucked in a breath. "Is she choking?"

"This isn't part of the show." Lavern threw the door open and rushed into the room.

Jinky and I darted in behind her.

Just as we reached the table, Annie dropped to the floor . . . unconscious.

"Is Annie okay?" I asked when Jinky stepped back into the waiting room at a nearby hospital.

We'd come here a couple of hours ago, following the ambulance.

Paramedics—after they'd managed to pry the octopus from Annie's face—had tried to revive her. But she was still unconscious when EMTs had taken her away.

Thankfully, she had a pulse. But her skin had turned a sickly pallor that made me nervous.

Not long after we'd arrived here, the Savannah PD had questioned us and taken our statements on what had happened. I was surprised they'd shown up, but maybe that was just standard procedure with an incident like this.

The two officers still lingered farther down the hallway. I wasn't positive, but I thought I'd seen one of them talking to a doctor earlier.

Anxiety thrummed inside me as I listened to all the familiar sounds of the hospital—sounds I couldn't stop hearing. Sounds that reminded me of when Phil had been rushed into surgery after his car accident.

Hushed voices. Rubber-soled shoes on linoleum floors. Beeps. Food carts rattling as their wheels turned. Papers rustling, and keyboards clicking.

Each sound made nausea churn in my stomach.

Jinky paced the gray floor in front of some stiff fake-leather couches that had been arranged in neat squares. "I don't know if Annie is okay. They don't know anything yet. I don't understand what happened."

By all appearances, Annie had choked on that octopus.

I didn't say that.

But the explanation was the only one that made sense.

"I'm so sorry," I murmured. "I'm praying."

"Where's Lavern?" Jinky glanced around as if she'd just remembered that Annie's assistant had ridden here with us.

Lavern had been crying the entire time. Crying so much that I worried about her own well-being, especially when she began mumbling incoherently. But she seemed to pull herself together as soon as we were inside the hospital.

"She went to the bathroom a few minutes ago." I pointed down the hallway to the Women's Restroom sign. "She's still very upset."

Jinky wiped her forehead. "I finally got in touch with my sister, Nancy—Annie's mom. She's on her way here from Texas. I just can't believe this. Why aren't the doctors telling me anything? Shouldn't they know something by now?"

When she stopped pacing, I put my arm around her shoulder. "I'm sure they will when they figure out what's going on."

She squeezed the skin between her eyes. "What a nightmare."

Just as she said the words, I heard footsteps in the distance. Heard someone say Lavern's name.

I turned around in time to see the two police officers in the hallway were moving.

Holding onto Lavern.

My eyes widened when I saw them escorting her away.

I grabbed Jinky's arm as we both watched in horror.

Wait . . . did they think Lavern had done this? What if what had happened to Annie wasn't an accident?

CHAPTER
TWO

AS SOON AS Lavern glanced at me with a desperate look in her eyes, I knew I had to do something. She wasn't much older than my own daughter, Scarlett.

From what Jinky had told me, the girl's mom lived in Florida. Her mom wasn't going to get here quickly, and Lavern needed someone to watch out for her in the meantime.

I looked back at Jinky.

But before I could say anything, she nodded toward Lavern. "Go with her. I'll wait here with Annie."

I nodded, relieved to have her blessing. I really didn't want to leave my friend in her time of crisis. "Keep me updated if you can."

As I rushed toward the hospital exit, I fished my

phone from my purse, found the ride-share app I used, and submitted a trip request.

It was a long story, but I didn't drive anymore. Times like this, I wished that wasn't the case.

But I didn't even have a car, and I couldn't do anything to change that fact at this moment. Right now, I just needed to get to the police station ASAP.

I saw the cop cars disappearing down the street just as another car drove up. I verified it was my driver before hopping in the back and telling him I needed to get to the police station as soon as possible.

Ten minutes later, we pulled up to the precinct.

At the front desk, I explained who I was and then paced the lobby as I waited.

I knew the cops had no obligation to let me see Lavern, especially since we weren't related, and Lavern was legally an adult. But if they could at least let Lavern know I was here, maybe she would find some comfort in that.

Maybe I could help in some way—I wasn't sure how exactly, but somebody needed to be here for her.

I continued striding back and forth, the sleeves of my cardigan pulled below my hands. At least my pencil skirt, blouse, and heels made me look professional. Maybe that would be a plus and would make someone take me more seriously.

The noises around me made my head spin.

Ringing phones. Murmured conversations. Quick steps.

Down the hallway, I heard an argument—it sounded like someone had been arrested who claimed innocence. Someone else smacked their gum. Another person in the waiting room played a game on their phone, the beeps and blips coming from the tiny speaker nearly sending me over the edge.

I tried to ignore the sounds as I paced. It was more than an hour before someone called my name.

Detective Garrison.

A whoosh of relief filled me when I saw his familiar face. The man was in his early thirties, with a square face and dark hair. He had a quiet demeanor, but he'd done a decent job solving cases in the past.

I knew from previous encounters with him that he'd be willing to help me. Police work wasn't my area of expertise, yet I'd been thrown into it several times, and I'd helped Garrison solve some crimes.

But, with my hearing abilities, I thought sometimes that he didn't know how to take me.

That was okay. I didn't always know how to take me either.

He offered a curt nod and kept his voice professional as he said, "Ms. Blackmore would like to see you."

I nodded, probably a little too quickly. But I didn't want to miss this opportunity.

I followed behind Garrison as he wove in and out of various desks in the office area until we reached an interrogation room located down a hallway at the back.

He paused at the door and turned to me. "You have five minutes."

"Thank you." I hoped the detective heard the sincerity in my words. I knew he didn't have to do this.

I swallowed hard before grabbing the doorhandle and twisting.

When I stepped inside the dimly lit room, I spotted a tear-torn Lavern sitting behind a table. The good news was that she didn't have handcuffs on.

Maybe they were just questioning her, not processing her into the system.

"Thank you for coming." She sniffed, her nose so red that it matched her hair. "I called my mom, and she said she's talking to a lawyer."

I carefully lowered myself into the metal chair across from her and squeezed her hand. "Everyone needs somebody in times like this. I'm glad I can be here for you. How are you holding up?"

More tears formed tiny rivers down her cheeks.

"I'm horrible. The police think I hurt Annie. I would never do that. I'm not that kind of person."

My thoughts raced. "Why in the world would they think you caused this? Annie just choked on the octopus, didn't she?"

Lavern shook her head. "That's not what they implied to me. Apparently, the ER doctor at the hospital told them that Annie didn't pass out from asphyxiation. She had some kind of toxin in her system."

"What kind of toxin?"

"The police believe I switched out the harmless octopus for a more deadly one, all because I secretly had a vendetta against her."

"Why would they think that?"

"They found out about the threats someone was sending Annie. Did you know about those notes?"

I nodded. "Jinky told me about them."

"The police think I was the one threatening her."

Lavern had said so much with those statements that I was going to need to dissect each fact one by one.

I licked my lips, trying to remain sensitive. "Let's start with the octopus. I assume you checked it before serving it to Annie?"

"Of course." The words came out emphatically. "I mean, I don't know much about them, but I ordered one that was edible when eaten alive. That octopus never left my sight after I picked it up."

I still squirmed at the thought of eating a living creature. "Do they think the octopus was venomous and bit her? Or was it poisonous—meaning, if she ate it, it would cause her to get sick?"

I'd just read an article distinguishing between the two.

"I'm not sure," Lavern muttered. "I didn't see any bite marks on her face, but I was also panicking when everything happened. And that octopus was still stuck to her face so . . ."

"Where did you get it?"

"At an Asian market not far from here—The Oriental Grocer."

I stored the name away in the back of my mind before moving on. "Why would the cops think you were the one who sent Annie those threats?"

Any way I looked at it, the explanation didn't make sense.

Lavern frowned and let out a shaky breath, as if she was holding back another sob. "Apparently, Annie had decided to report the threats a few days ago and, when she did, she mentioned my name. I have no idea why. I had nothing against her. I didn't want to see this happen. How could the police even think this? How could *Annie* even think this? I don't understand."

I didn't either. And I didn't have much time here to find out everything I needed to know. Apparently, Annie hadn't told Jinky she'd gone to the police. I wondered what had caused the change of heart.

"Did Annie give the police a copy of the notes?" I asked.

"I have no idea. But they brought me in fast, almost as if I was already a suspect." Lavern stared at me, hope and despair clashing in her gaze.

I had to agree with her. The police had acted fast. They clearly knew something I didn't. Maybe even something that Lavern didn't.

But what?

This girl's grief seemed real. So did her fear.

I leaned closer and lowered my voice. I didn't want to do this, yet I knew I had to.

This girl needed some help, and I knew I was in a position to offer that. I couldn't look the other way.

"Look, if you'd like, I can ask some questions," I told her. "I can see if I can find out what's really going on here."

Lavern stared at me, gratitude in her gaze. "Yes. *Yes!* You would do that for me?"

I rested my hand over hers. "I'd be more than happy to."

She squeezed my hand. "Thank you. Thank you so much. I've been so scared."

"Anyone in your shoes would be."

Her gaze met mine. "Am I going to be okay?"

I wanted to reassure her. I wanted to say yes. But I knew I couldn't do that. I had no idea what the outcome of the situation would be.

"I'm going to do everything I can to help you," I finally told her. "I promise you that."

As I finished that statement, the door opened. A brisk, petite man wearing a business suit strode inside. He had thinning gray hair, a pinched expression, and wore small, wire-framed glasses.

"Lavern Blackmore?" He paused. "I'm Lewis Nester, your lawyer."

"My lawyer?" She straightened. "Did my mom call you?"

"She did." He glanced at me dismissively. "You can leave now."

Before I could respond, an officer led me out.

But my thoughts remained on the situation.

What had really happened to Annie King?

Knowing there was nothing else I could do here, I stepped outside the station into the balmy spring heat and called Weston Turner.

Weston was a country music superstar, my first love, and a current instructor at the Grand Isle Music Conservatory. I hadn't known when I accepted the job offer that the man who'd broken my heart all those years ago was now employed by the school.

We'd had our ups and downs, but at this moment we were friends. Maybe more than friends. I wasn't sure exactly. But we'd definitely been enjoying each other's company over the past several months.

It just so happened we were supposed to have dinner together this evening. Not necessarily as a date, but we were learning to possibly trust each other again.

Weston answered on the first ring. "Hey, gorgeous."

His voice had a lingering Southern drawl that always made my knees a little weak.

"How are you?" he asked.

I glanced at the various cop cars parked around me and remembered how today had gone completely sideways. "I'm . . . okay."

"I can tell by your tone that something is wrong."

I let out a quick sigh before giving him a brief update on the situation. Then I paused and asked, "Any chance you could pick me up here at the police station?"

"Of course. I'll come get you, and then we can do an early dinner. Does that work? Or do you need to go back to the hospital?"

"I'm going to call Jinky and see how things are going. I can let you know."

"Either way, I'll be right there."

I ended the call, grateful to have Weston back in my life.

I dialed Jinky's number next. My normally gregarious friend sounded subdued. Worry had a tendency of doing that.

"How's Annie?" I paced closer to the building and out of the direct sunlight.

"The same. My sister is on her way. As you can imagine, she's very upset." She paused. "How's Lavern? Did they arrest her? What's going on?"

I nibbled on my lip as I tried to decide exactly what to say. If I told Jinky about the poisonous octopus, she might also think Lavern was guilty. I didn't want to throw more fuel onto the fire. But I didn't want to lie either.

"Lavern is upset, but her lawyer is with her now," I finally said. "Hopefully, he'll get everything sorted out."

"At least that's something. I'm guessing they brought her in because she was the last one to handle the octopus?"

I swallowed hard. "That makes the most sense. I'm sure they're trying to cover all their bases."

"Lavern's mom has money. That's a good thing, I suppose. It always seems to help people—in my experience."

I shifted as I heard Jinky's voice waning. "Listen . . . do you need me to come sit with you?"

"No, I'm fine. Jeff is here with me now."

Jeff was a guy Jinky had met a couple of months ago, and they were now dating. I'd met him once, and he seemed decent enough. He was an engineer, divorced, and quiet.

"Oh, and I just forwarded screenshots of those notes. I'd still like you to look into them . . . just in case."

"Sounds good," I told her. "I'll check in later."

As soon as I ended the call, I looked in my inbox. Sure enough, Jinky had sent me those screenshots. The messages were just as she said. All typed. Clever sayings.

But I had a feeling these weren't playful.

Had someone done this to Annie on purpose? And, if so, was it the same person who'd sent these threats? Was there any possibility Lavern was behind this?

That's what I needed to figure out.

CHAPTER
THREE

AN HOUR LATER, Weston and I were sitting at a restaurant on River Street in Savannah.

Since the spring evening was temperate, we'd picked a table outside. The small space inside was a little too echoey for my tastes. At least outside, the noise had a chance to breathe, to disperse, instead of simply bouncing off the walls and into my ears.

On a street corner a block away, a man with a saxophone played a lonely tune while people dropped change into his instrument case. A group of ladies loaded with shopping bags passed us, giggling as if they'd had too much to drink. A riverboat glided across the Savannah, its paddles slopping water and humming as passengers stood at the railing and waved to onlookers.

Weston and I had ordered tapas for our meal, and

we were sharing our selections. I'd gotten stuffed mushrooms and garlic shrimp. Weston had wanted to order calamari, but I convinced him not to. Even though the squid he wanted to eat was already cooked, I couldn't get the image of what happened to Annie out of my mind. Instead, he'd ordered a cheeseboard and mini crab cakes.

He'd picked me up and, before coming here, we'd swung by The Oriental Grocer. The place had been closed, however. I'd have to pay another visit tomorrow.

I stared across the table at Weston—at his barely there beard. At his brown hair that was flecked with red. At his trim, cowboy-worthy body—even though he wasn't truly a cowboy. Still, he wore those fitted jeans, boots, and a cowboy hat like a pro. And when he sang, people forgot that he'd actually grown up in suburbia.

He had the swagger, the looks, and the voice to be a star—and he was one.

I waited until we got to the restaurant to give him the full rundown on everything that had happened earlier today.

"That's crazy." Weston shook his head as he grabbed a piece of Swiss cheese from the board in front of us. "But I'm glad that you could be there for

Jinky—and this Lavern girl. It sounds like God put you in the right place at the right time."

I liked his way of thinking. Time had been both good and bad to us both. Bad in that we'd had to learn lessons we'd rather not learn. But good in the sense that those lessons had helped us to grow and mature.

I let out a long breath, realizing that I was dominating the conversation. "Enough about me. How are you?"

He glanced at his plate, and I knew something was on his mind.

Instantly, tension crept up my spine. I could read people enough that I knew when bad news was coming. I'd been in my fair share of situations like this before.

I wasn't going to like whatever he had to say.

He shifted. "My record company wants me to go on tour again. I'm right up at the end of this semester at Grand Isle. I'm trying to figure out if I'd rather continue working here or if I want to get back on the road."

He'd stopped touring so he could spend more time with his kids. His ex-wife, Athena, had moved with them here. I admired the fact that Weston was trying to be a good dad. He'd given up everything to be a part of their lives—which had been increasingly difficult lately now that his ex was dating Pete Hedgesworth, a bad boy rock and roll singer who brought drama wherever he went.

But how did touring fit into Weston's overall plan?

And, on a lesser note, how did touring fit into our future?

My heart pounded at a steady, almost doom-filled tempo in my ears. "What are you going to do?"

"I'm not sure yet. It's a lot to think about."

"You've got a lot of talent." I needed to busy myself with something, so I picked up a cracker and broke it in half.

The world—at least, the part of the world that liked country music—was waiting for Weston Turner to reemerge on the music scene. His fans missed him. Concert venues missed him.

He was a first-rate act, a natural entertainer who had the audience in the palm of his hands.

Weston's gaze locked with mine. "You could come with me. We could do a reunion tour. People would love that. My record company already threw the idea out there after that video of you and me singing at the Christmas concert went viral."

The students at Grand Isle had convinced the two of us to do a duet.

To say it had been a smashing success would be an understatement.

I shook my head. "I'm not interested in that kind of life."

"You do have the summer off. Don't forget that." He tilted his head and gave me a hopeful glance.

I nodded slowly, even though I still knew what my answer was.

But I also knew what touring could mean for us—even though there wasn't officially an "us" yet. I wasn't sure our growing relationship could survive him going on tour again.

After all, that's where our relationship had fallen apart last time—more than twenty years ago.

"You're immensely talented." I wiped my mouth before placing the napkin back in my lap. "If going on tour is what you want to do, then you should."

I felt like this was a replay of our younger days. In fact, the words I just said might be the exact ones I'd told him two decades ago—back when both of our futures had seemed so bright, and the world seemed like an opportunity before us.

"Camryn . . ." Weston reached across the table and squeezed my hand. "I know this is a lot to think about."

"That's why we're keeping things easy, right?"

Tension strained my voice. I wasn't ready to jump into anything. That's why we were taking our time.

Or, I should say, *I* was taking my time.

His gaze locked on mine. "But what if I didn't want to keep things easy?"

My breath caught in my throat. What did he mean by that?

I wanted to ask him. But, at the same time, I didn't.

I hadn't dated much since my husband died—just a few dinners here and there and one awkward kiss.

Which made me think I wasn't ready yet.

I tried to figure out what to say, how to respond.

Before I could, my phone rang. I didn't recognize the number even though the area code was local.

My thoughts went back to Lavern. What if she was calling?

I excused myself and put the phone to my ear.

But it wasn't Lavern on the other end.

It was my father.

I ended my phone call with my dad and looked across the table at Weston. "I hate to cut this short but . . ."

"I wasn't trying to eavesdrop, but was that your

dad?" Weston studied my face, waiting for my confirmation.

I nodded, still feeling the waves of shock coursing through me. "Apparently, he's out of prison."

"What? I thought he was serving a life sentence."

Life sentence? Yes. That's what James Theodore Paine should be serving since he'd ultimately cheated people out of approximately twenty million dollars.

"I thought so too." My voice cracked. "You know how that goes. Overcrowding. Good behavior. Winning appeals."

Weston offered a half eye roll. "I've heard. Where is he now?"

I swallowed hard, still in disbelief about the words that were about to leave my lips. "That's the thing. He said he had a taxi driver drop him off at my apartment."

Weston's eyebrows shot up. "He's there now? How does he even know where you live?"

"I sent him a Christmas card this year, and I believe my return address was on the envelope. I should have known better. Anyway . . . that's why I said I had to cut this short. I'm going to need to go talk to him." Dread pooled in my stomach. It had already been a hard day. Seeing my father was only going to make things worse.

"Of course." He pulled out his wallet and dropped some bills on the table.

Then Weston escorted me out to his truck—a black F150—and we started down the road. As we did, my thoughts raced.

I needed more time to prepare before seeing my dad. Something like this just couldn't be thrown on me, not after all these years.

My dad had gone to prison because he was a con artist. He could sell sand to a desert dweller.

To just say we had a strained relationship would be an understatement.

"Do you want me to stay with you?" Weston glanced at me, quickly studying me with his gaze before looking back at the road.

I didn't have to consider his question for long before nodding. "I'd love that. If you don't mind."

"Of course. I'd be more than happy to."

Weston had met my dad while the two of us dated in college. That was before my dad had been arrested for "selling" government owned beachfront properties to unsuspecting buyers in North Carolina. He'd conned people out of their life savings—and that hadn't been his first rodeo.

My father had never liked Weston—probably because Weston could see right through him. The couple of times I'd brought Weston home with me on break, we'd always ended up leaving early because of the tension.

Weston wasn't the type to be taken advantage of —even if he was trying to impress his girlfriend's father. I'd admired that.

Finally, we pulled up to my apartment building.

I wished I didn't feel a rumble of nerves as I stared up at the three-story brick structure. Normally, this place was my refuge, where I came to unwind and reflect.

But tonight, it wasn't. My apartment was now a place with the potential to inhabit bad, unwanted memories concerning my father.

I let out a breath.

It was time to face my past.

And I wasn't sure I was prepared to do so.

I SLOWED my steps when I saw a man wearing a coat and fedora leaning against the wall beside my apartment door. James Theodore Paine.

"Dad . . ." I paused, tension immediately pulling between my shoulders.

He straightened as a grin stretched across his handsome face. Yes, handsome. People always said he looked a little bit like Richard Gere, and they were correct. The two definitely had similarities.

Even after all these years in prison, Dad had barely aged. Maybe there were a few more wrinkles. Maybe a little less dark hair—it was hard to tell since he wore a hat.

But it appeared he'd come out on top—as he always did.

"Camryn . . ." He shook his head as he stared at

me, something that looked vaguely like warmth and affection in his gaze. "You are still gorgeous. Just like your mom."

I swallowed the lump in my throat.

My mom had died during childbirth, so I'd never met her. But I *had* met the four other women my father married after her death—all beautiful, affluent, and in want of my father's complete attention. None of them had desired an add-on daughter as they'd been wined and dined by my dad.

He'd always claimed Mom was the only woman he'd truly loved. He said it with a wistfulness in his voice that made me wonder if he was telling the truth. However, it was hard to trust anything my father said.

His gaze wandered beyond me. "Weston . . . this is unexpected. Camryn didn't tell me the two of you were seeing each other again."

I crossed my arms. My dad and I hadn't spoken in ten years—ever since he'd reached out to some friends of mine from prison, soliciting them for money because he was dying of cancer and the state wasn't paying all his medical bills.

He wasn't dying.

The whole story had been fake.

That's when I'd stopped visiting him.

Bile churned inside me at the thought.

An intrinsic part of me thought I should be more loyal. But I'd learned through years of therapy about the importance of setting boundaries. Forgiveness didn't always mean reconciliation.

I cleared my throat. "I haven't told you anything in a decade. And Weston and I are . . ." I glanced back at him, trying to encapsulate our relationship.

It wasn't that we were *just* friends, but it wasn't that we were more than that either.

"You don't have to explain." My father clamped his hand down on Weston's shoulder. "It's good to see you, boy."

Funny that it didn't matter how old you were . . . to the older generation you were always a child.

"It sounds like we have a lot to talk about." I nodded at my door. "Would you like to come in?"

"I thought you'd never ask."

Fighting a sense of dread, I ushered him inside. After he was seated in an armchair by the window and I got him something to drink, Weston and I both sat on the couch across from him.

I expected a moment of awkwardness to fill the air.

But not with my dad.

My dad was the life of the party. The one who always knew how to make conversation. And some things just never changed.

He rambled on and on about my apartment, my past music career, Scarlett.

But I knew we needed to get down to business. I had some serious questions I needed answers to.

"You're out . . ." I started. "No probation?"

"None. What can I say?" He shrugged good-naturedly before winking. "I had great behavior. Of course."

In other words, he'd charmed the entire system. Again, that wasn't a surprise either.

He swished saliva in his mouth, as he always did when he was thinking.

Probably no one else heard it. The sound was subtle.

But I knew he was waiting for the right moment to say something. My dad believed that not only was timing everything, but that the right delivery could mean success or failure.

Finally, my dad looked at me and said, "I was hoping I might be able to crash here for a while."

Instantly, my heart beat harder.

I opened my mouth, wondering how I could refuse my dad a place to stay. It didn't seem very loving to turn away family.

But still . . .

I wrestled as I tried to form the right words, as

my sense of compassion collided with my boundaries.

"How about you stay at my place?" Weston's voice cut into my thoughts. "It's bigger."

My eyes widened as I glanced at him. Had he really just volunteered to do that?

He *had*.

Gratitude filled me—undying, unwavering gratitude.

Weston was my hero right now.

"I hate to put you out." Reluctance marred my father's voice—not because he didn't want to put Weston out. My dad *loved* feeling like the world revolved around him. People changing their plans to accommodate him probably made him feel important.

Dad's reluctance was probably all for show.

"It's no problem," Weston said. "But I need to get back home soon, and I hate to rush you . . ."

My dad grinned at me. "That's okay. Camryn and I have plenty of time to catch up. Don't we, sweet pea?"

"Plenty of time?" The words made my throat ache as they left my lips.

Wasn't that what most people wanted with their aging parents? More time?

But most people . . . they didn't have a dad like mine.

Once Weston and my dad left, I collapsed on the sofa, my thoughts racing.

What a day.

First, everything that happened with Annie. Then Lavern had been taken in for questioning. Then Weston had told me he might go back on the road. Now my dad had been released from prison and showed up on my doorstep.

I really hoped this was it for today.

My head dropped against the couch, and I wished I would be content just to sit here. But I knew I wouldn't, not when I had so many things to work out. To solve. To fix.

Wasn't that what moms did? They tried to fix things.

That's what I certainly tried to do. If there was a way I could help, then that's what I did.

Scarlett was finishing up her freshman year of college. She was studying business, and I'd yet to hear what her plans were for the summer. I anticipated a call from her anytime.

She was welcome to stay with me, but I had a feeling she'd rather discover the world, take sailing lessons in the Caribbean, or explore the Canadian Rockies with some friends while traveling in a camper van.

A part of me would like to go with her.

Especially now that my dad was back in the picture. Getting away for a while didn't sound like a bad idea.

I shoved those thoughts aside and, out of curiosity, grabbed my computer. I typed in "ASMR," and a list of videos popped up.

I found one with more than a million views and began to watch.

Here in my apartment by myself, I could freely cringe and squirm all I wanted as I listened to the amplified sounds of someone noisily eating.

I *really* didn't understand why some people enjoyed watching this, why they found it satisfying. It just grossed me out.

I played several of the most popular videos before finding Annie's channel.

She was up there with some of the best of them. As I watched her videos, a thought hit me.

Lavern had been recording Annie today. After each dish Annie had eaten, she'd sent the videos to Annie's computer as well. It wasn't a live feed.

Instead, the various camera angles would be sliced and diced into a final product.

That meant there were at least two copies of the footage.

No doubt the police had taken one.

But I wondered if I might watch the other. I wasn't sure what I hoped to find. But there could be *something* there.

The idea seemed worth a shot.

After a moment of hesitation, I dialed Jinky's number. She still sounded subdued as she answered.

"Any updates?" I started, pulling a blanket around me—not because I was chilly but because I needed some comfort.

"No, not yet. Nancy—my sister—just got into town about an hour ago. We're still hopeful that Annie will pull out of this."

"I've been praying for that," I told her. "But I have a question. I hate to ask you now with this going on, but . . . is there any way I can get my hands on the video that was taken today? The one that was sent to Annie's computer?"

"I . . . I don't know. But I can see what I can do."

"If you have a chance, do that. I'd like to watch what happened again."

She paused. "Wait . . . do you think Lavern did

this? Do you think this was something other than an accident?"

I swallowed hard, trying to choose my words carefully. "I don't know what happened. The doctor told you that she didn't choke on the octopus, right?"

"That's what I thought I heard him say. But I was certain he was wrong. That's the only thing that makes sense."

"I know what you're saying . . . but the cops are saying that Annie ingested some kind of toxin." I didn't mention that the toxin could have been from the octopus itself.

"Toxin?" Jinky gasped. "No . . . how can you accidentally ingest a toxin?"

I swallowed hard again. "That's what the police are trying to figure out. In the meantime, I wanted to watch the video, just in case I can find some answers."

Jinky let out a long, labored breath. "If I can get it to you, I will. But it probably won't be tonight."

"I understand. Just as soon as you have the chance."

I had a to-do list for myself tomorrow. I would visit that Asian seafood market. I would hopefully watch this video. And I would figure out what to do about my father.

CHAPTER
FIVE

ALL NIGHT I had dreams that involved slurping and chewing.

It was a nightmare that replayed itself over and over again.

When I looked in the mirror the next morning as I got ready for work, I saw the exhaustion in the circles beneath my eyes, the dullness in my gaze, and slight lines around my lips—frown lines.

I'd woken up with one conclusion.

I needed to talk to Professor Skittles.

Professor Skittles really wasn't a professor at the music conservatory where I worked. She was actually my assistant and someone who'd legally changed her moniker to Professor Skittles. Her personality was just as colorful and bright as her name.

I wasn't disappointed when I walked in and saw her already seated at her desk.

Her workspace had just as much personality as she did. The filing cabinet behind her was covered with knickknacks and bobble-headed anime figures. Ink pens with artificial flowers taped onto the ends were arranged in an old vegetable can that had been plastered with stickers.

I'd always thought that Skittles with her colorful outfits and oversized platform shoes could be a character on a TV show. Oftentimes, she donned suspenders or knee-high socks or headbands with cat ears.

She was basically an anime come to life.

She also always carried her trademark fruity candies with her wherever she went. She often separated the colors, and whichever one she was eating at the time proclaimed her mood for the day.

I glanced at her desk and saw a small bowl of yellow candies.

Good. Yellow meant she was happy.

"Good morning." I stopped by her desk and leaned my hip against it. "I have a question."

Her head popped up in surprise, and that's when I saw her AirPods.

She hadn't heard me coming.

"I didn't do it," she blurted.

"Do what?" I squinted.

"Nothing." Yet guilt seemed to stain her face. "It's just my standard response. Just ignore me."

I shook my head, trying to get my thoughts back in focus. "Listen, what do you know about these ASMR and mukbang artists?"

"You know what mukbang is?" She twisted her shoulders and looked at me out of the corner of her wide eyes. "I'm impressed."

"I only heard about it yesterday for the first time so don't be too impressed."

She stared in the distance a moment before shrugging. "I know a lot of people are really into it. As you know, I'm fascinated with Korean culture—K-Dramas, to be specific. But mukbang really started there, and it's recently spread to the US."

"Like many things Korean." K-Pop, K-Dramas, and now mukbang.

Working here at the college had taught me a lot.

"Speaking of which . . . I saw the video," Skittles blurted.

"What video?" I crossed my arms and stared at her, having no idea what she was talking about.

"The one where Annie King tried to eat the octopus."

I froze. "What? How did you see that?"

"It went up on her channel this morning. It's been all over social media how she almost died. How the octopus almost choked her."

I didn't correct her. "Who would have put the video up there?"

"People with these channels usually have a team behind them—so I assume someone who works for her did it. There's a note at the end of the video asking for prayers for Annie and saying that any funds monetized from that video would go to her medical care."

"I guess that's nice." The words didn't even feel right coming out of my mouth. Who would want their near-death experience to be online for anyone to see? Did Jinky know about this?

And . . . who had put it online? Not Annie. Not Lavern.

So, who?

"Do you want to see it?" Skittles asked.

I'd been hoping to get a link from Jinky to see this but since it was already online then I guessed I didn't need that.

Part of me dreaded seeing it happen again. I didn't want to see someone almost lose their life. But I needed to. I wanted to see if I might have missed anything.

I pulled my chair up beside her and nodded. "I do."

She started tapping at her laptop. "Do you know Annie or something?"

"As a matter of fact, I met her yesterday."

Skittles sucked in a breath. "Yesterday?"

"I was there when all this happened."

She stopped typing and turned to me, giving me her full attention. "Really?"

"Yes, really."

"What was it like to witness it? Was it gross?"

"You do know she's at death's door right now and her family is really worried?"

Skittles sobered. "Right. Sorry. I can only imagine."

I nodded at the laptop. "How about that video?"

Most people covered their lips when their mouth dropped open in horror.

Not me. I covered my ears.

I'd moved a chair beside Skittles and sat behind her desk. She tapped her keyboard and, a few seconds later, I saw Annie. Annie with her dark hair perched in that tight ponytail atop her head. Annie looking totally clueless about how her life was about to change. Annie who thought she'd hit the jackpot when she discovered the art of eating online.

I watched as the camera focused on the octopus squirming in her bowl. Watched as she picked it up. As its arms clung to her fingers.

That was hesitation in Annie's eyes, wasn't it?

She was taking greater risks in order to get more views.

Were her choices born out of desperation? Or was it simply human nature to want more, to want to go further?

Just as I remembered her doing, Annie stared at the octopus a moment before raising it to her mouth. The creature looked normal—not that I knew a lot about octopi. But nothing stood out about it. It was probably ten inches long.

What had ever happened to it? Had the police taken it in for evidence? Were they checking to see what type it was, if it could be the kind that's poisonous to humans?

Annie put a tentacle in her mouth and chewed. Then she sucked in a breath.

I heard fear in the sound. Heard her desperation for more air.

Each sound was amplified by the strategically placed microphones.

I watched the footage twice before I asked Skittles to close her laptop.

I couldn't view—or listen to—the video anymore.

But I did have Skittles send me a copy just in case this episode got taken down, which I suspected would happen in lieu of the investigation—or maybe even out of common decency.

"Pretty sad, huh?" Skittles shrugged. "Maybe she should've thought twice about eating that live octopus. You know what I say. If it moves, in your mouth it shouldn't groove."

"You really say that?"

"Who doesn't?"

Anybody else on the planet. But I didn't say that. Instead, I shifted my thoughts. "I don't think eating the live octopus caused her reaction. I think there was more to it than that."

Skittles gasped before popping a yellow piece of candy into her mouth, almost acting as if it were a piece of popcorn and she was enjoying a good movie. "You're looking into it, aren't you? I want to help. What can I do?"

I raised my hand to slow her thoughts. "I'm not rushing into anything. But the police may or may not have a suspect, and I may or may not have said I wanted to see if I could find out something for her."

"You're so good at investigating. Just think about what happened with the Abernathys."

I'd been asked to help the Abernathys—an affluent local family—find the contents of their home after everything had been loaded into a moving truck, which had then disappeared. I'd been hesitant to help, but thankfully everything turned out okay.

"Just because I've solved a couple of crimes, that doesn't make me an expert," I reminded her.

Skittles shrugged as if she didn't believe me, remaining unfazed. "So, what are you doing now?"

I resisted a sigh, trying not to overthink this as I leaned back in the stiff chair beside Skittles. "I need to check on Jinky. Then I'm going to pay a visit to the Asian market where Lavern purchased that octopus. If Annie didn't choke on it, and it was instead a poisonous, inedible variety, I want to know."

Skittles' eyes lit. "Can I come?"

I thought about her offer a moment before nodding. I *would* need a ride. And Skittles and I could talk strategy about some work projects on the way.

"Okay," I told her. "You can come. But give me at least thirty minutes before we leave. Sound good?"

She grinned. "Sounds *muy bien*—or should I say —mukbang?"

I groaned.

What was with all the jokes revolving around that word?

It didn't matter.

I had other things to think about.

Like attempted murder.

CHAPTER
SIX

JUST AS I finished talking to Jinky—there were no updates on Annie yet—I started back to my office and ran into Weston.

As in literally.

I collided into him as I rounded a corner.

He reached for me and caught my shoulders to steady me. As my gaze locked with his, I sucked in a breath.

After all these years, he still had that effect on me.

"Distracted?" Amusement danced in his hazel eyes as he studied me.

"You could say that. Sorry." Immediately, my thoughts veered from the electricity racing through me, to Annie, and then with another jolt of anxiety I asked, "Where's my dad?"

"I left him at my place." Weston shrugged.

"What?" Panic crawled through me. "That is a terrible idea. You can't leave him there alone."

My hands went to my temples, and I rubbed them, worst-case scenarios rushing through my head.

"What's your dad going to do at my place that has you so worried?" Weston asked the question slowly, carefully.

"You don't know my dad. Those guitars you have hanging on the wall, especially the one that's so special to you—and valuable?"

A knot formed between Weston's eyes. "What about it?"

"My dad is the type of person who will sell the instrument to the highest bidder and then replace your guitar with a fake so that you never know."

Weston twisted his head, looking at me like I might have a screw loose. "I think you might be over-thinking this."

I shook my head, my panicked thoughts still racing at a frenzied pace. "You have no idea what he's capable of, especially if he's desperate for money. He obviously came here to Savannah because he wants something. He could have gone anywhere. But he came here."

"Maybe he truly wants to make amends with you."

I let out a skeptical chuckle. "No way. There's more to it than that. There always is."

"Camryn . . ." Weston glanced around as if to make sure nobody was nearby before stepping closer and running his hand up and down my back in a soothing manner. "This doesn't even sound like you. You're always calm, cool, and collected."

"Not when it comes to my dad." I barely heard his words—and I definitely wasn't living them right now. "Dad has this weird hold over me. I thought he walked on water until everything went down. Now, I don't even know what to think of him."

"Anyone in your situation would feel that way."

I jerked my gaze up to meet Weston's, trying not to melt at the compassion in his voice.

I'd been on my own for three years now . . . and I wasn't used to people being this concerned for me.

I swallowed the lump in my throat. "I don't want him to steal from you."

"Camryn . . . calm down. Nothing's going to happen at my house. I'll be careful."

Again, I barely heard what Weston said. Or I did, but I quickly moved on, knowing he was talking nonsense. "I'll find him another place to stay. Maybe there's a cheap apartment somewhere he can rent. I'll even pay for it myself if I have to."

"Camryn . . ."

When Weston didn't say anything else, I finally met his worried gaze.

"Just take a deep breath," he murmured. "You'll figure this out. I know you will."

There was so much I wanted to say to him. So many ways I wanted to argue and tell him he was wrong.

But I didn't. Not right now. Besides, I'd told Skittles I would meet her, and I was already late.

And I was *never* late.

"I have to get to class." Weston took a step back. "We can catch up later?"

I nodded, liking that idea. "That sounds good."

But as I went to find Skittles, my thoughts continued to race.

A bad feeling brewed in my gut.

Brewed like a storm in the distance heading my way.

A very destructive storm that I could only take shelter from—but that I knew I couldn't stop.

"Have you ever been to an Asian market?" Skittles chatted a million miles a moment as she drove to The Oriental Grocer.

Apparently, Skittles loved visiting places like this.

I barely listened to her babble. Chaos wreaked havoc inside my head. Usually, I was good at weeding out the sounds around me so I could function like a normal person. But every once in a while, noises got the best of me.

Right now, on top of Skittles talking, I heard the rotation of the tires. Heard cars zooming past. Car horns occasionally honking. Heard the colorful tassels Skittles had hanging from her rearview mirror swishing together. Heard the soft clang of her hoop earrings as they dangled from her ears.

With each new noise, my anxiety wound tighter.

Finally, we pulled up to The Oriental Grocer—and not a moment too soon.

I needed to get some fresh air and regroup my thoughts.

The good news was that the store was open right now, unlike last night when Weston and I stopped by. The building was square and composed of concrete blocks that had been painted yellow. The name of the store had also been painted in black over the doors. There was nothing fancy about the place, from its appearance to the grass growing in between the cracks in the parking lot.

As we stepped inside, an extra loud bell jangled overhead.

Usually, the sounds around me were the first thing I noticed.

But here, it was the scent of seafood—an aroma I found to be repugnant.

My gaze went to the man behind the counter. He was thin and short with graying hair and oversized plastic-framed glasses. A dirty black apron stretched across his front side, and he held a knife—possibly a cleaver—as he expertly chopped some type of seafood.

His nametag read "Haruto."

"Excuse me." I stepped toward him. "I was hoping you could help me with something."

"I *didn't* have anything to do with the girl's *incident*." His words came out quick and brisk, and he barely even made eye contact.

I tried not to be taken back by his reaction. "I take it you've already had people coming in here asking questions."

"The *police*. *Reporters*. Online *social media* people."

"I'm sorry to hear that. I can only imagine how frustrating that might be."

"I am almost ready to *close down* for the day. But I can't *afford* to *lose* the business." His cleaver hit the wooden cutting block with more force than necessary.

My throat tightened—not because I felt like I was in danger, but because he seemed so adamant.

He slowed his chopping and glanced at me. "What do *you* want?"

Diversion was a great PR tactic. Maybe that's what I'd just done—although it came naturally to me. But my understanding of his emotions was sincere and not a ploy.

"I'm just trying to find out information about that octopus. I'm friends with Annie King. I'm not here to try to drag you down or rake your name through the mud. In fact, based on what you tell me, we could clear your name."

He stared at us skeptically. "Who are you? Just *friends*?"

"This is Camryn, and she's amazing," Skittles interjected. "She's so good at solving mysteries."

Skittles then proceeded to tell Haruto in detail about the two other mysteries I'd solved since moving to Savannah.

To my surprise, Haruto nodded, seeming to listen with interest to every detail Skittles shared.

"My *seafood* is top *quality*." He practically spat out the words, emphasizing the importance of his statement.

"So, there's no way the octopus killed her?" I clarified.

He began chopping, maybe even more furiously, if that was possible. "The most *dangerous* part about the *octopus* is the *possibility* of having it *suction* to your throat and *choke* you. I told them that. There is only *one* poisonous octopus that is dangerous for humans to eat—the blue-ringed octopus, which looks very *distinct*. I do *not* carry it. I inspect *everything* that comes through here *myself.*"

"Good to know." Haruto's statement left no room for questions. "Is there anything else that stood out to you about this purchase?"

"If you ask *me*, you need to talk to the tall, skinny, red-headed girl who *bought* it."

"Lavern?" Her name left my lips before I could stop it.

"I do not know her *name*. All I know is that she was *acting suspicious.*"

"Suspicious how?" My pulse pounded harder.

I was supposed to be helping Lavern, not pointing a finger at her. But I needed to know all the details so I could be one step ahead of this.

"She was on her *phone* the whole time, and she talked as if something was wrong. But as soon as that *other girl*—the one who is in the *hospital*—came around, she ended the conversation as if she were *hiding something.*" He raised his cleaver, jabbing it in the air each time he emphasized a word. "*She* is the one you need to look at. It would *not* surprise me if she was up to *something*."

Skittles and I exchanged a look.

That didn't sound good.

Apparently, I needed to talk to Lavern again.

But that would be more complicated considering she was still being held by the police. At least, I assumed she was. Jinky hadn't said otherwise.

I needed to find out. I didn't have her number, so that would be more complicated.

But I did have one idea.

CHAPTER
SEVEN

"*SO, WHAT NOW?*" Skittles asked as soon as we were back in her car.

Her intonation mirrored Haruto's—on purpose, no doubt.

"We should probably get back to work," I reluctantly told her. "We have those new summer programs to advertise as well as the end of the year commencement concert."

Thank goodness, I wasn't involved with this event like I had been the Christmas concert back in December. Weston and I had emceed that event—and sang a duet at the end. This time, I was only in charge of publicity.

For the longest time, I'd been known as being a fixer. It was what I did. Whenever a company had a problem, the board came to me, and I figured out how to put a PR spin on their issues for them.

I never did anything unethical. But sometimes, companies got a bad rap for no good reason—just because a few strong-willed people got angry at them. That's where I came in.

When I came to Grand Isle Conservatory of Music, the college was in dire trouble. There had already been one murder. Enrollment was down, as were endowments. But, even if I had to say so myself, I'd done a pretty good job restoring its reputation in the seven months since I'd arrived. We'd received some great press over the past several months. Win, win, win!

"There *is* one other person I want to talk to," I muttered, thinking out loud entirely more than I should.

Skittles rubbed her hands together like she was a squirrel about to discover a huge acorn before quickly grabbing the wheel again. "Who?"

"Lewis Nester, Lavern's lawyer. It'll be easier to talk to him than it will be to talk to Lavern. I want to hear if there are any updates. I'm not sure he'll tell me anything, though."

"Well, you never know if you don't try, right? And practice makes you presentable."

"Perfect," I said. "It makes you perfect. Anyway, I

can search for his business address. What do you say?"

"I say let's do it." Excitement stretched through her voice.

I quickly found out where Nester's office was located. Thankfully, it wasn't too far away. We headed there, parked, and strode toward the door.

As we did, I tried to compose myself.

Even though Skittles didn't think so, pretending to be a private investigator was a whole new world to me. I wasn't a hundred percent confident about my abilities.

But I was going to do my best.

I pulled open a heavy glass door. This place was the opposite of The Oriental Grocer—perfectly laid out with no expense spared. The people who worked in this building wanted everyone to know they were wealthy.

"I'll take the lead," I told her as we stepped inside.

Then I prayed I'd have the right words and not blow this.

Mr. Lewis Nester glanced up at me, already annoyed, and I hadn't even said anything.

"What can I do for you?" His voice sounded brisk and impatient.

His secretary had told us we had three minutes.

What was it with people giving me time limits? First, Garrison yesterday at the station, and now this. Either way, at least I had the opportunity to talk with Nester.

He evidently thought highly of himself—that was clear by his expensive office and clothing.

How had Lavern's mom afforded to hire him? Unless her family came from a lot of money also.

"Yesterday—" I started.

Before I could even finish, he finished for me. "That's right. At the police station. Yes, I'm representing Lavern. Lavern gave me permission to speak with you. But that still doesn't tell me what you're doing here." He twirled his finger in the air as if trying to fast forward through this, and his voice almost sounded mocking.

"Rude much?" Skittles muttered beneath her breath.

As a mom who wanted to teach people manners, I felt like I should correct her. But the other part of me didn't care. The man kind of deserved the snide comment because he was being so boorish.

"Lavern asked me to help her," I started, shifting in my seat.

Nester pressed his lips together, and his eyelids drooped as if I was boring him. "You do realize I charge a hundred thirty dollars for a consultation, don't you? You need to get to your point because otherwise I'm going to start timing this, and you'll be racking up your bill."

My hands went to my hips as I stared at him. While I didn't mind if people were professional and brisk, I *did* mind when they talked down to me. "Lavern asked me to help her. How is she doing?"

He shrugged lackadaisically. "As well as to be expected, I guess."

"When will she be released? They can't hold her more than forty-eight hours, right?"

"They actually can. She's being charged with attempted murder."

I sucked in a breath. So, the police weren't *just* holding her anymore? They'd actually pressed charges?

Urgency pounded in every heartbeat.

"There's enough evidence for that?" I'd seen the video myself. I'd been there when it happened. And nothing about this seemed like a slam dunk.

Nester shrugged again. "She was the one who handled the octopus, and therefore who had the most opportunity to switch it out. Lavern also posted something on social media about wanting to kill Annie."

I sat up straighter, uncertain if I'd heard him correctly. "What?"

He smirked. "Social media will be the death of this country. Mark my words. If young people are smart, they'll stay far away from those online sites before their lives are destroyed—just like my client's life has been destroyed."

I bristled. It seemed as if he'd already given up on Lavern's case.

"Where did she post she wanted to kill Annie?" I asked. And why hadn't I heard about this? That seemed like something that would be pretty important to mention.

I suppose Jinky didn't know, which meant Annie must not have told her.

Was that because Annie wasn't concerned? Was it because Annie didn't want her aunt to be concerned?

I didn't know.

"She posted something on ChattySnap—*Some days are amazing and other days I'd like to strangle my boss.* She said it was a joke. She even took her post down. But it was too late. People took screenshots of what she said and reposted it."

"What did Lavern say?" Skittles' intense gaze

latched onto Nester's, and she made it clear the man didn't intimidate her.

"Ms. Blackmore said she made the comment in a moment of frustration, and that's why she removed it just as quickly. She said she didn't mean the words, that what she wrote was simply an expression. But it's like I tell my own kids: words matter. It's good advice for you two also." He flicked his finger between the two of us as if he were our uptight, self-righteous grandfather.

This guy was giving me whiplash, and all we were doing was talking.

I swallowed hard, knowing Nester could go off on a tangent about nearly anything I asked him.

But I still had questions.

"We heard that the cause of poison was *not* the octopus, however," I started. I didn't know that officially, but that's what Haruto indicated. I was going to latch onto that theory and see where it led.

Nester narrowed his eyes as he studied me. "Then you've heard more than I have. I haven't heard anything official except that Ms. King was poisoned."

"Isn't there any way you can get Lavern out of this?" Skittles asked. "Especially if she's not guilty."

His expression remained placid. "It's not my job to figure out whether or not she's guilty. It's my job to keep her from being convicted."

I already didn't like this guy. Where had Lavern's family even found him? Then again, he was probably the type who got results.

I suppose when it came to situations like this, that was what someone wanted. It's what I would want for Scarlett. But there had to be a way to balance this all, right? A way to have integrity along with justice?

"I'm still not sure why you're here." Nester offered us a cold stare, acting as if he were a king, and Skittles and I were his servants.

That made me not like him even more. I was all for living with humility—but I wasn't going to let others put me down.

I narrowed my eyes, feeling *really* irritated. It irritated me even more that I was getting irritated because I didn't want him to affect me, and he was.

"What's your strategy?" I knew he had no obligation to tell me—even if Lavern had given him permission.

His beady gaze met mine. "Do you really think that I'm going to tell you that?"

"I was hoping you would, especially since I only want to help."

"You want to help?" He let out a mocking laugh. "I don't need your kind of help. You might be a PR expert, but you're no lawyer or investigator."

Anger burned through my blood. "I'm sorry you

feel that way. But I'm more than competent, whether I have some bloated degrees behind my name or not."

I nodded toward the diplomas on his wall.

"Is that right?" He still sounded unconvinced and almost mocking.

"You may have a great track record in the courtroom, but in the court of public opinion, you're an unlikable, arrogant man."

He stared at me a moment, and I didn't know how he would react.

I didn't know where my words had come from—only that they were true.

Finally, he let out a laugh. "I've got to hand it to you—you've got moxie. I've read about you."

"Read what about me?" It was my turn to be surprised.

"That's right. I do my research. I know you helped solve those other two crimes in the area—the first at Grand Isle and the second with the Abernathy family. I also know who your husband was."

I swallowed hard at the mention of Phil. If Nester even tried to pull any punches or insult Phil in any way . . .

Nester sighed. "If you must know, we have another suspect we're looking at."

"Who?" Skittles leaned closer as if anxious to

hear, as if watching a tennis match and waiting for the next play.

He let out another long sigh. "Ms. King's ex-boyfriend has the best motive. That's all I'm going to tell you. Anything else you want to know you're going to have to find out on your own. I don't need any amateur detectives distracting me. Do I make myself clear?"

Oh, he was clear all right.

If I had my way, I'd never talk to this guy again.

SKITTLES and I were out of time, so we headed back to the college.

I couldn't justify taking off the entire day, especially since I was getting paid to work at Grand Isle. Although, I had to say, I'd put in entirely enough overtime hours that I *shouldn't* feel guilty. Still, it had been bred into me to be responsible.

The thought reminded me of my father again.

He was the one who'd taught me to be responsible. How ironic was that?

He'd never pressured me to be like him. In fact, he'd taught me to be the *opposite* of him. When I'd run a lemonade stand once, I remembered running low on the drink. I'd wanted to water the liquid down to stretch it further, but my father insisted that I give everyone a quality product. So, I had.

My head pounded at the thought of my mixed-up childhood.

I thanked Skittles once we got back, and then I immediately headed to Jinky's office. Jinky was a voice professor here at the school, and she'd once been a part of the Sydney Opera House.

I wasn't sure if she'd be in today or if she would be at the hospital, but I wanted to double-check.

To my surprise, she was behind her desk grading some papers. Today, she wore a bright pink poncho over a black pantsuit, and her blonde hair was swept up in a twist that formed something that looked like a fountain atop her head.

Without invitation, I slipped inside and shut the door for privacy. Then I lowered myself into the seat across from her.

"How are you doing?" I studied her face and noted the wrinkles around her eyes. She was clearly concerned—as anyone would be in this situation. Despite her outfit, she didn't look nearly as perky as usual.

"I didn't sleep very much. It's hard watching people you love suffer." She waved a hand in front of her eyes, as if the action might dry up any coming tears.

"Yes, it is. I was really hoping Annie would turn around overnight."

"We all were." She pulled out a tissue and dabbed her eyes.

I shifted, trying to be sensitive. I wanted more information because I was a concerned friend, but also because I needed answers.

I tried not to get her emotions stirred any more than necessary. This was where investigating felt tricky.

"Jinky, I have a few questions for you if you don't mind. I want to figure out how Annie was poisoned. If it was an accident or if someone could have possibly done this on purpose."

"Whatever I can do to help." She wadded up the tissue but left it on her desk.

"I heard Annie was dating someone, but that it ended badly."

Her eyebrows shot up as if she was surprised. "That's right. Desi Samms. He goes by the name Desi Does online."

My spine straightened. "Desi Does?"

"Desi, like Desi Arnaz from *I Love Lucy*. He's also a performance artist, and that's the name on his online channel."

"And what does Desi do?"

Jinky drew in a deep—but shaky—breath. "He started by doing eating competitions and stuff. But he got really sick once and didn't want to do that anymore. Instead, he jumped on this new trend of 'subscribers decide.' So, for example, he'll ask his subscribers what he should eat the next day. If he gets a certain number of responses, he'll eat the menu they come up with. His subscribers have decided what he wears, what he does, etc."

That sounded miserable to me, but what did I know? "Someone told me that people suspect him in what happened to Annie. Do you know anything about that?"

She let out a long sigh. "I know he and Annie had a bad breakup. But I have a hard time figuring out how he would have somehow tampered with her food to do this. Plus, I just don't know if he would take it that far."

"Is there any way I could get in touch with him?"

Jinky shrugged. "You can try. He's a local. But, from what I understand, he's MIA."

"What?" My eyebrows shot up. "That's suspicious."

"I know. That's what I thought too. It just makes him look guilty." Jinky shrugged as if she didn't know what else to think about that.

"How long has he been MIA? Since the video yesterday?"

She nodded. "That sounds about right. He usually posts about three videos a day on his channel. But he hasn't posted any since Annie's . . . incident. Could it be because he's upset? Maybe. But if he's upset, then why isn't he answering his phone? Apparently, he's not at his house either. He lives here in Savannah, and I sent Jeff over to tell him face-to-face what happened. He didn't answer. One of the neighbors said Desi's place was quiet all night."

I shifted in my seat, trying to be sensitive about the situation. The last thing I wanted was to make this worse for my friend. Desi could just be on a break or he could have taken a trip. Still, this apparently wasn't his MO. A lot of these YouTubers publicized every detail of their lives online.

"I'm really sorry to hear about that," I started. "Can you tell me anything else about Desi? Why did he and Annie break up?"

She let out a long breath. "I never got good vibes from the guy. He seemed like the type who just wanted attention and would do whatever it took to get ahead. He would sacrifice *whoever* was needed in the process, if you catch my drift. He left Annie about six months ago for another YouTuber, a woman named Celeste Matheson."

I took a mental note of her name. "Who is Celeste?"

Jinky began fanning her face using the papers she'd been grading. "All I know is that she surpassed

Annie in views. She didn't even start posting until after the two of them broke up. Annie always thought Desi had shared Annie's secrets with Celeste in order to help her get ahead."

"Secrets?"

Jinky shrugged. "Upcoming episode ideas. She had her videos timed and edited for the most impact —it took a lot of trial and error to come up with that strategy. To figure out what people liked for her to eat. How to angle the microphones just right. Her episodes look easy, but they actually take a lot of thought."

Celeste definitely sounded like someone I needed to check out. "Where does this Celeste live?"

"In Charleston, actually. So not too far away. But she and Desi broke up so . . . I don't know."

At least Charleston was close. It would be easier to talk to Celeste that way. "Did Annie have any other enemies?"

"Besides Desi and Celeste?" Jinky thought about it before nodding. "There's also an assistant she fired a couple of months ago—Penelope Jenkins."

"Why did she get fired?"

"I don't know. Annie would never share that with me."

I stored that name away. "One more question.

What about Lavern? How long have they known each other?"

"All I know is that Lavern started out as a fan, and then Annie ended up befriending her and then hiring her. The two of them seemed to get along well. Annie never said anything suspicious that would make me think that Lavern would be behind this."

"Did Annie ever say anything about a threat Lavern posted online?"

Jinky blanched. "A threat? No. What are you talking about?"

"Apparently, Lavern posted something about having the worst boss or something. She said it was just an off-handed comment and that she didn't mean anything by it. But it's one of the reasons the police are looking at her now."

"I can't imagine she would have meant the words . . . she and Annie seemed to get along so well. Then again, I don't know much about the woman."

Neither did I. That needed to change.

Especially if I wanted to find out any answers.

Back in my office, I pulled out my favorite snack— carrots with mustard. The combination sounded weird, but it was a perfectly healthy snack with a great crunch factor.

I caught up on some correspondence at the office and had a brief meeting with Chancellor Joseph Hannon.

But as soon as I had the chance, I pulled up YouTube and watched the Desi Does videos.

They were just as ridiculous as I thought they might be.

Desi seemed to be trying really hard to be entertaining, but there was something not quite right with his delivery. He just didn't have one of those naturally entertaining personalities. It was almost like he tried too hard—and the extra, unnatural effort showed on-screen.

Then I found Celeste's channel.

Celeste seemed like a natural entertainer, the kind of person who could make anything sound interesting. I wasn't sure that she was better at the mukbang stuff than Annie, but she was definitely entertaining.

The girl had white-blonde hair, overly tanned skin, and wore white eye makeup. Everything she did was exaggerated and intense, often with the camera slowly zooming in on her eyes to the end shot.

However, something about her also seemed insincere. I didn't want to make a snap judgment. But I instinctually didn't like her.

I clicked on Celeste's most recent video, one she'd posted just this morning. This one wasn't about eating, but about Annie.

Tears glistened in Celeste's eyes as she mournfully told viewers what had happened. Then she announced she was planning a vigil that evening for Annie at one of the city parks here in Savannah.

As soon as I finished watching, I took a mental note of the time and place. I was supposed to have dinner tonight with Weston and my father.

Was there any way I could do both the dinner and the vigil?

I nibbled on my lip a moment.

I felt certain that Weston would be okay with me heading out early for the vigil. In fact, part of me was tempted just to skip dinner altogether and avoid seeing my father. But that wasn't the way I operated. Even if I didn't like conflict, avoiding it would be immature.

Out of curiosity, I searched for Celeste's address, but I couldn't find it. So, it seemed that if I wanted to speak with her, I would need to catch her tonight.

I'd figure out a way to make it work. If I could avoid my father in the process, then that would be even better.

At that thought, my phone rang. It was my neighbor, Mr. McClements. I answered, curious because the retired lawyer hardly ever called me.

"Hey, Camryn," he started. "I just wanted to let you know that I saw a suspicious car drive past today. They stopped in front of the building and took a picture of your apartment."

"How do you know it was mine? There are a lot of apartments in our building."

"It was clear the camera was pointing directly at your place."

"Did you get a look at their face?"

"No, sorry. I only saw the camera lens coming out the window. It could be a fan or . . . it could have been someone else. I just thought you'd want to know."

"I do. Thanks, Mr. McClements."

"Stay safe, Camryn. This is a crazy world we're living in."

I couldn't deny that.

CHAPTER
NINE

AT THREE O'CLOCK, Jinky stuck her head through the doorway into my office.

"Lavern was just released on bail," Jinky announced.

I straightened, surprised at how cheerful she sounded—especially considering that Lavern was a suspect. "Is that right?"

Jinky nodded. "Lavern's mom and Nancy have been talking—mother to mother. Nancy doesn't think Lavern is guilty either. Anyway, Lavern is at home now, and she asked if she could talk to you. She doesn't have your number."

"I would love that."

That's how twenty minutes later I ended up in the car with Jinky driving to the apartment where Lavern lived, which thankfully wasn't too far away. The place wasn't in a great part of town, but I'd seen worse.

When we stepped inside, my gaze went to the mismatched decorations and piles of junk dotted across the room.

Lavern clearly wasn't a neat freak.

But when I spotted her on the couch, I forgot about the mess.

Especially when I saw her tears.

She'd just been through a horrible ordeal—and it wasn't over yet.

I glanced into the kitchen and saw a woman in her fifties standing there, a hand over her mouth. I could tell by her profile that she and Lavern were related. They both had the same prominent nose and high cheek bones. Except whereas Lavern looked gawky, this woman's features made her look uniquely beautiful and almost exotic. Her clothes also looked designer—beige linen pants, a rich-looking black shirt, and strappy sandals.

Instantly, I wondered about the family dynamic. About where Lavern's father was. About their possible affluence.

The woman stepped forward. "I'm Julie. I understand you're helping my daughter."

"I'm willing to do whatever I can. But I'm not an expert or anything."

She pressed a fist over her mouth as she glanced at Lavern. "I just can't believe any of this. It's so horrible. What if my daughter goes to prison?"

"We're trying not to let that happen," I told her, hearing the near panic in her voice.

"Thank you . . . I really appreciate it."

Julie nodded toward her daughter, and I went to sit beside Lavern. I put an arm around her shoulders and let her cry. As I did, Jinky stood beside Julie, and the two of them spoke in low tones.

"Thank you for coming," Lavern said softly, her voice trembling.

"Of course. Was there any reason you needed to see me?"

"I was hoping you could help me. I don't know how . . . but I'm desperate."

"I'll do whatever I can." I shifted. "But I'll need to ask you a few questions."

Lavern straightened, as if pulling herself together. "Whatever you need to know."

I removed my arm from around her. "How did you meet Annie?"

Jinky had told me, but I wanted to hear her version.

She pulled her blanket up higher on her shoulders. "I was a big fan. When I saw her doing a public appearance in Charleston, I went to meet her. Afterwards, we started talking and became friends. When Penelope left, I volunteered to help with her show. Two weeks later, Annie hired me. I have a degree in film, so I know how to put together a video. I think she liked that I had some experience."

"I have one more thing I need to ask," I told her. "I heard that when you went to go pick up the octopus from the Asian market you were on the phone, and you didn't seem very happy about something. What was that phone call about?"

Lavern's eyes widened as if she hadn't expected me to ask that question. Then she shrugged. "I don't know what you are talking about."

I didn't believe her. Not for one minute.

I tilted my head, my gaze latched onto hers. "Are you sure about that?"

"Positive. That guy who worked there was old. Maybe he doesn't remember very well."

In honesty, Haruto was probably ten years older than me. Funny how age was subjective like that. He didn't seem old to me.

I continued to stare at Lavern, still not believing that she didn't remember anything. "Maybe. Are you sure you weren't on the phone?"

"I'm sure. If I was, it was probably just about something inconsequential, something I don't even remember."

Lavern could think that all she wanted.

But I knew she was hiding something. I could tell by the catch in her voice.

There were certain advantages to having super-sonic hearing—and being a human lie detector was one of them.

Jinky dropped me off at Weston's.

Dread pooled in my stomach the entire drive there. I did *not* want to see my dad again. I didn't want to force any awkward conversations or pretend I cared when I really didn't.

Except I knew I did.

He was my father and, no matter what he did, we were connected for life.

Despite my hard feelings, I could learn to be cordial.

I knew all these things were true in theory. I only hoped to sincerely live them out in my life.

I paused before knocking on the door to Weston's humble abode.

Yes, *humble.*

He'd won multiple CMA awards, had platinum albums, and songs that had topped the Billboard charts. In other words, he had plenty of money. He even had a mansion waiting back in Nashville. I was pretty sure he hadn't sold it since I'd heard him talking to someone about maintenance on it not long ago.

So, I had to admire the fact he lived in a somewhat ordinary house in a mostly ordinary neighborhood. Despite his fame, nothing about him was flashy.

He'd told me once that he just needed enough space for him and his kids when they came to visit. That's what he had—a neat and cozy bungalow.

Weston's eyes warmed when he opened the door and saw me standing there. He leaned forward and gave me a quick kiss on the cheek.

I flushed as I felt his lips brush my skin.

I didn't want to admit it, but I loved any attention I got from Weston. I'd always been that way. He had the ability to make me feel as if I were the most important person in the world to him.

But I'd made the mistake of believing that once. If I believed it again and he let me down, then I would be a fool. I was forty-four years old now, and I didn't want any romantic drama. I just wanted peace. Was that too much to ask? Could I pursue love and simultaneously have harmony in my life?

I wanted to say yes, but I wasn't sure.

Even though he'd given me a good reason as to

what had happened when I thought he'd cheated on me, it was still hard to separate myself from my emotions about it all. We'd taken a break, which Weston had thought meant we'd broken up. He met someone else in the meantime, fell in love, and got married.

I'd been crushed.

All those feelings disappeared as soon as I saw my dad standing behind Weston.

A huge grin stretched across Dad's face, as if me seeing him was the most normal thing in the whole world. Somehow, he was wearing nice new clothes. The pants looked expensive with their crisp lines, the shirt bore a designer label, and his shoes looked like genuine leather.

Where did he even get that outfit? I really hoped Weston hadn't bought anything for him.

"If it isn't my favorite daughter," my father crooned, his arms outstretched as if I might hug him.

I had no desire to do so.

"Your *only* daughter," I reminded him, giving him a quick cheek-to-cheek hug instead.

But I *wasn't* the only child. However, Joel—my brother—wasn't one to put up with my father's stunts.

Speaking of which, I needed to contact Joel. But

the last time I'd spoken to him, he was in the Middle East doing some type of security work.

I really needed to follow up to see where he was working now, but it was so hard to stay on top of his schedule.

"Everything's ready to eat," Weston told me. "We were just waiting for you."

"It smells wonderful in here." And it did. Sizzling meat along with what I guessed to be garlic bread filled the air and made my stomach rumble.

In the rush of today's schedule, all I'd eaten were those carrots with mustard.

If I knew Weston, he'd made steak, potatoes, and bread. He was a Texas boy through and through. Even though he'd grown up in urban Dallas, he was still somehow a cowboy.

After we sat down and prayed, I tried to think of something normal to talk about with my father.

Instead, my gaze went to the guitars hanging on Weston's wall.

Were those really Weston's treasured guitars? Or had my father pawned one of them and used the money to buy himself new clothes and then replaced the instrument with a replica?

Weston caught my gaze and gave me a look. He knew exactly what I was thinking.

I wondered if he'd checked out his guitars after

our earlier conversation. I hoped he'd taken me seriously.

I'd have to address that later, however. Right now, I wanted to enjoy this meal, even if my father was here with me.

CHAPTER TEN

WE WERE ONTO DESSERT AND, so far, dinner hadn't been nearly as unpleasant as I thought it would be.

My father had talked some about his time in prison. Told me how he'd traded his food for nicer clothes and grooming items. I had no doubt he'd weaseled his way to the top of the food chain there and had somehow ended up with a whole protection detail in his prison network.

It sounded just like my father.

"So, I overheard a conversation earlier." My dad shifted before shrugging. "I wasn't trying to overhear, but you know . . ." He shrugged again. "Sometimes you just hear what you hear. It sounds like you're investigating something."

"When would you have heard that?" The question popped out of my mouth before I could stop it.

"When I ran to the restroom, I heard you two say something about poisoning and going to ask people questions." He shrugged. "I just put it together."

When he went to the restroom? I was going to have to be more careful.

Not much slipped past my father.

"That's right," I reluctantly told him. "It turns out I actually have a pretty good eye for solving mysteries. Or an ear for it, I should say."

He chuckled as if that was the funniest thing he'd heard in days.

"I always knew that you could do whatever you set your mind to," he said, his voice deep and soothing—one I'd cherished as a child. "Although, I have to admit, I was hoping it would be music."

I cringed. My dad had tried to convince me to go full-time and pursue music with everything I had in me. He'd used every tactic in his arsenal. He'd told me how much better my life would be. How I'd never have to worry about money. He'd try to act as my manager and had set me up with interviews without telling me in advance.

But a full-time career in music wasn't what I had truly desired, despite any talent or looks for it that I might have. People found it weird that I'd walked away from something that so many people wanted.

All I'd wanted was normal. When I had met Phil, I realized that he offered me everything I desired. The chance to have a family. To remain quiet and build a private, stable life.

Most people still didn't understand that.

"So, what are you investigating?" My father cut off a piece of his steak with flair, reminding me of a character in a soap opera.

I hesitated and exchanged a glance with Weston. When he gave me a slight nod, I figured that was the encouragement I needed to share. I told him the details of what had happened, figuring this was a safe enough conversation.

I mean, at least it wasn't personal.

I finished telling my dad the details just as I took the last bite of my cheesecake—one that Weston had picked up from my favorite bakery in town. I liked it plain with no chocolate or fruit on top. Cheesecake by itself was simply perfection.

Weston had remembered that, a fact that got him bonus points in my book.

My father put his elbows on the table and leaned toward me. "I know where I'd start if I were you."

I froze, not sure I wanted to hear. "Where?"

"You look at the person with the biggest payoff.

That's what it comes down to—love and money. In most cases, it's a mixture of both." He said the words with absolute authority.

Of course, one of the reasons he'd gotten away with so many of his cons was because of his ability to read people. Maybe I'd gotten some of that from him.

But, despite my feelings about my dad, he could have a point.

I thought about his words a moment, and I wondered which "player" had the most at stake.

My thoughts stopped on one person. Or maybe two.

Celeste and Desi.

I glanced at my watch.

That vigil for Annie started in thirty minutes. I could still get there if I left now.

"You have someone on your mind, don't you?" A glimmer of satisfaction sparkled in my dad's gaze.

I nodded. "I have a chance to talk to this person, but I'd have to leave now."

"Then what are you waiting for? Get out there and find some answers. Make your old man proud."

Make him proud? It wasn't on the top of my to-do list.

But I didn't need to tell him that. Not right now.

The vigil was taking place at Forsyth Park in Savannah, right in front of the beautiful fountain at the northern end of the area. Live oaks draped with moss towered around Weston and me, and fragrant azaleas dotted the landscape with pink and white flowers.

Celeste didn't stand on a platform. Instead, she'd set up near the fountain.

All around her, people had their cameras out, recording every moment of what was happening. If I had to guess, probably forty people had shown up.

I'd also spotted two cops there.

Were they for crowd control? Or were they scoping out any potential suspects?

I wasn't sure.

Celeste had started by handing out Annie's favorite snack to people around her—fried crickets with Old Bay seasoning. They were served in little plastic cups with Annie's picture on the front.

On the surface, the event all seemed very touching and sincere. The crowds around me certainly seemed sad. There were tears in their eyes as people held pictures of Annie, many of them screenshots from videos she'd made. Not all the photos were flattering—not to me anyway.

But maybe in the mukbang world, they were acceptable. Annie's head had been photoshopped and placed on colorful, mostly fluorescent backgrounds. There were snapshots of her face with her mouth wide open as if about to insert food. Other ones, her cheeks were full as if she'd just taken a huge bite. Another had her looking upward as if delighted by something in her mouth.

Weston leaned closer as we stood on the edge of the crowd. "What do you think about all this?"

I kept my eyes on everyone around us. "My original opinion still remains."

Celeste didn't strike me as authentic.

If my dad's theory was right, then Celeste and Desi had the most to gain—which therefore put them at the top of my suspect list.

But what about Lavern? What did she have to gain? Did she secretly want to be a YouTuber? Were her loyalties divided?

I wasn't sure.

But I was missing something.

I scanned the crowd again. "Desi's not even here. I think that says a lot."

Weston followed my gaze. "Maybe he's also a victim. You said he's been missing since Annie's video was made, right? So at least twenty-four hours?"

"That's right. So, he's either a victim or a suspect. It's too early to tell."

Just then, a few fans stopped by and asked for Weston's autograph. He cheerfully gave it to them, careful not to draw any more attention to himself than necessary.

Weston was good like that.

He always had been.

When fame first hit him, he'd eaten it up. I thought his popularity had changed him. And it may have for a while. But Weston seemed to have come back to a nice center of gravity. A *surprising* center of gravity.

He'd married Athena Roland—a formerly highly sought-after fashion model. They had two kids together: Allison, who was fourteen, and Tyler, who was twelve.

Athena had left Weston for a filthy rich tech mogul. She'd then dumped the tech mogul for Pete Hedgesworth. I'd met the rock star before, and he gave me all kinds of bad vibes.

"Me standing here watching her isn't really going to do anything to help me," I mumbled to Weston. "As soon as this is over, I need to talk to her."

"You don't expect her to open up, do you?"

"No, that's the tricky thing. Trying to get information willingly from someone isn't as easy as it sounds." Working public relations, I'd learned the art of sharing only pertinent information that reflected the image we wanted to project. It wasn't rocket science. People did that all the time—some even did so expertly.

"I'm here for you, whatever you want," Weston said. "You just let me know."

Gratitude filled me. I was really glad Weston was here with me right now. I needed to figure out exactly where our relationship was going. It wasn't fair to him to keep him hanging.

He'd told me I could take as much time as I needed to figure things out. So that's exactly what I was doing.

But for now, I needed to pay attention to Celeste.

I needed to figure out what happened to Annie. And the answers could very well be here right now.

CHAPTER
ELEVEN

AS SOON AS the vigil ended, people surrounded Celeste.

She ate up the attention, engaging with each person around her with overblown expressions and reactions.

I wanted to believe her tears were sincere, but I still had trouble doing that.

Was I being judgmental? Or discerning?

There was a fine line between the two it seemed.

I waited patiently.

For now.

Eventually, I was going to have to weave my way over to her to talk. But currently, throngs of fans listened to her every word.

Finally, fifteen minutes later, I saw my opening.

Celeste's eyes met mine, and she smiled as if she expected me to gush.

Then she saw Weston, and her gaze widened. "Wait . . . Weston Turner? I can't believe you're here. I'm such a huge fan. Do you want to be a special guest on my show?"

Of course, she recognized him.

He was especially noticeable when he wore his cowboy hat and boots. Tonight, he'd traded that for a baseball cap and Nikes. I appreciated the fact that he was trying to be inconspicuous.

"I'm a *huge* fan," she repeated as she turned to Weston.

She paused almost as if expecting him to say that he was also a big fan.

"Thank you," he said. "I'm sorry to hear about your friend."

"I appreciate that." She lowered her head. "We're all torn up over it."

"I can imagine." Weston shifted. "By the way, this is my friend Camryn."

Celeste turned to me, her gaze still assessing.

She recognized me too, didn't she?

I hadn't been nearly as famous as Weston, but I'd had my flash-in-the-pan moment of fame.

Or maybe she recognized me from somewhere else . . . this investigation maybe? Was she the one who had taken a picture of my apartment? Was that because I was with Annie when she was poisoned, and Celeste was now trying to keep an eye on me?

I needed to keep that in mind.

"I've heard you sing. In fact, I love the two of you together. I'm truly honored that you're both here." She made a heart with her hands and placed it on her chest.

I swallowed hard, not really enjoying the fact I was about to burst her bubble. "I'm actually a friend of Annie King."

Her eyes widened, and she took a quick step back as numerous emotions battered her gaze. Surprise? Fear? Grief?

I wasn't sure.

"Wow. I didn't realize that," she finally said. "Well, I'm really sorry to hear about what happened to her. I would *love* to chat more, but I have other people waiting to talk to me right now and—"

Weston moved to the other side of Celeste, blocking any fans who tried to get to her. It would be hard for her to talk to anybody but us. I was okay with that.

"Tell me a little bit about your relationship with Annie." He crossed his arms.

Celeste's eyebrows shot up. "I didn't do anything to her if that's what you're asking."

"That's not what I said." Weston kept his voice unaccusatory—for now. "I was just wondering what your relationship is like."

"Annie and I respect each other as professionals." She raised her chin.

"What about Desi?" I asked. "I heard he dumped Annie to date you, that the two of you teamed up and stole Annie's ideas in order to overthrow her as the current US queen of ASMR."

Celeste sucked in a breath as if my words surprised her. The reaction only lasted a couple of seconds—but long enough for me to see it.

"Desi Does? I don't really want to talk about this anymore." Celeste glanced around as if looking for an escape route.

"If you don't have anything to hide, then what's the big deal talking to us?" I continued to press.

Celeste looked up, her gaze still shaken. "This whole thing has me spooked, okay? What if I'm next?"

"You think someone has a hit out on mukbang artists?" Weston clarified.

She nearly flinched at his words. "I have no idea what to think. I'm still not even sure exactly what happened to Annie. Was she poisoned? Was all of this on purpose? Or was this just a near fatal mistake she made?"

"Why don't you start by telling us what you think?" I suggested.

"I don't know. If I did, I would tell you."

"Who do you think might be responsible?" Weston asked. "If you had to pick?"

"If I had to pick? I'd be looking at Lavern Blackmore, the person the police have in custody."

"Why would you say that?" An edge of defensiveness rose in my voice, but I pushed it down.

"Because Lavern was my friend before she was Annie's assistant."

I was about to ask another question when fans broke through the blockade Weston and I had around her.

And I knew our conversation was over.

For now.

But that was okay because I had plenty to think about.

A few minutes later, Weston and I headed back to his truck. But as we passed a cluster of trees, I paused.

Someone huddled behind the trunks.

Someone familiar.

"Lavern?" I stepped closer, my voice nearly breathless.

"What?" Weston repeated, inching closer to me. "*Lavern* Lavern?"

I took another step forward, ready to ask questions or even chase her.

But I didn't have to.

Lavern stepped out, guilt stretching across her face. She motioned for us to join her behind the trees. "I don't want anyone to see me."

"Why not?" I asked.

"Because the people here might think I'm guilty. I just don't want to deal with it."

"Then why did you come?" I asked her.

"Because Annie is my friend, and I'm worried about her. I wanted to see who was here. See if there were any suspects or someone who might have done this to her." Lavern stared straight ahead and narrowed her eyes as she glared at Celeste.

Obviously, no love was lost between the two.

I still wondered exactly what had happened to have caused the tension between them.

"Did you see anyone suspicious?" I pushed.

"Just her." She nodded to Celeste, a certain iciness to her tone.

"Speaking of Celeste . . . she said something curious," I started. "She said that the two of you used to be friends."

Lavern's scowl deepened. "It's true. But I'd like to forget that part of my life."

"What happened?" Weston's voice hardened.

Lavern sighed and crossed her arms as if she didn't want to have this conversation.

"The two of us were friends, and Celeste was looking for the next big thing that was going to explode—chasing trends, I suppose," Lavern explained. "All she ever wanted was to be famous. It's what she lives for."

I waited for her to continue.

"Anyway, she decided to start her own channel, and she dropped me as if I'd never existed. That's what Celeste does. I've heard numerous stories of her doing the same thing to other people."

I continued to try to put pieces together. "How did that lead to you going to work for Annie?"

"What I told you earlier was true. I volunteered to fill in for Annie, and, after a couple of weeks, she offered me the job."

"How did Celeste feel about that?" Weston asked.

"She was furious. She said she changed her mind and wanted me to come back and work for her."

"Up until then she had no interest in ASMR?" I asked.

"That's right. No interest at all. Like I said, she was looking for the next big thing. When she realized how well Annie was doing, I think that's when she got interested in ASMR."

"Lavern, do you know how that video of Annie nearly dying got posted online?" I watched her expression carefully.

Lavern looked away, her shoulders drooping. "I posted it while I was at the hospital."

"Why would you do that?" Weston didn't bother to hide the confusion in his gaze.

"I knew that's what Annie would want. That's going to be gold for her. People will feel compassionate toward her about what happened. Then when she pulls through this . . . she'll really be a superstar."

"This wasn't a publicity stunt, was it?" I held my breath as I waited for her answer.

I didn't want to ask the question, but I had to know.

"Of course not! Annie likes ratings, but not like this." Lavern looked away again. "I went to the bathroom at the hospital and posted it. As soon as I did, I wanted to take it down. But I couldn't. The police came and brought me in for questioning."

"One more question." I scooted closer as a group of people who'd been at the vigil flooded by. "Who were you talking to on the phone at the Asian market? Don't tell me this time that you don't remember. We both know that's not true."

Guilt flooded her gaze. "You're right. But Annie's credit card was declined, and I was trying to sort things out. She gave me access to her finances so I could help her with that also. When I checked into that credit card, I discovered it was maxed out at ten thousand dollars. I have no idea what she spent that on."

"Why didn't you tell me that when I asked earlier?"

She shrugged. "I asked Annie about it, and she swore me to secrecy. She said everything was fine. She looked so serious . . . I could tell everything wasn't fine. But I didn't want to go back on my word."

WESTON and I were quiet as we sat in his truck, not going anywhere. Not yet.

He probably knew I was mulling over everything we'd learned. It was a lot.

"What do you think about all this?" I glanced at him, at the shadows that hit his face. At that profile that was so alluring. At his eyes that contained depth and feeling unlike any other man I'd ever met.

"I don't really know what to think—except that all this is a mess. I had no idea the stakes were this high, but people will go to great lengths to succeed, won't they? Not just in music—but in whatever field they're in."

"I'm trying to figure out where Annie was spending her money. From what I gathered from

Jinky, she was still living at home. So, in theory, Annie *should* have a lot of money in the bank."

He sighed and rubbed a hand over his beard before cranking his engine and easing onto the road. Country music crooned through the speakers, settling my nerves—just slightly.

"Hopefully, the police are following the money trail," Weston said. "They have a better chance at finding answers than either of us."

"I agree."

Another moment of silence passed.

"We were interrupted last time when we started talking about me going on tour," Weston started.

Anxiety pooled in my stomach—actually, it crashed there like a tidal wave. "I know. What do you think about it?"

"I'm not sure." He shrugged and stared out the windshield.

"How long do you have to decide?"

"Three days."

Three days? That wasn't much time. Not for a decision like that. "Going on tour again could change everything for you. But I thought you moved back here to have a more stable schedule and see the kids more often."

"I did." Weston frowned and rubbed his beard again. "But this tour would just be for the summer."

Just for the summer . . . I knew how those things turned out. The summer goes well, so dates are added. Before you knew it, you were on the road for a year.

Even if your best intentions were for a limited travel schedule, record label execs had a way of convincing people to see things their way.

I swallowed hard, trying to figure out how I felt and what I wanted to say. Finally, I settled on, "That sounds like a great opportunity."

"But you're a great opportunity also."

I blushed, not expecting his words. I didn't even know what to say. I didn't like acting like a high school girl with no experience. I'd been married before. I should have a better handle on these things.

But Weston had always held an unseen power over me.

I struggled to know what to say.

I licked my lips and glanced behind us. When I did, I saw the headlights there. They were closer than I liked. I kept watching, noting that whenever we turned, so did the car behind us.

Coincidence? I couldn't be sure.

"What are you thinking about?" Weston asked.

"I'm wondering if we're being followed."

Weston glanced in the rearview mirror. "That's a good question. Let's find out."

Weston made another quick turn. As he did, memories hit me.

Memories of the accident that had claimed my husband's life. For years, I'd blamed myself—even though another driver had hit us. But last year, I'd discovered there was more to that story, more to my husband's death than I'd ever imagined.

Still, it was too late. The damage was done.

My husband was dead, and I was forever immobilized by the thought of getting behind the wheel again.

Those memories came rushing back until my heart raced erratically.

I gripped the console in front of me, wishing I could disappear.

"Hold on!" Weston jerked the wheel to the right, and we rounded a corner.

As we did, his truck fishtailed, nearly drifting into oncoming traffic.

But it didn't.

When the truck straightened, Weston pressed on the accelerator and sped away from the car on our tail.

I glanced behind us.

The headlights appeared again.

We were *definitely* being followed.

But who would be following us right now? It had to be someone from the vigil. Celeste maybe? Or what about Lavern?

It didn't matter. Either way, I felt like an emotional wreck. Flashbacks continued to pummel me, and I was certain Weston and I were going to die. That another life would be claimed by an automobile.

"It's going to be okay," Weston muttered.

I wanted to believe that. But he was a country singer, not a former Navy SEAL. How was he going to get us out of this? He hadn't exactly taken defensive driving classes.

I pressed my eyes closed, unable to look anymore.

I felt him make another sharp turn.

I heard horns blaring around us.

I felt danger stretching through the air.

But I tried to block it all out.

Dear Lord, please help us. Protect us.

The good news was that I didn't feel any nudges. Maybe the person behind us was just trying to send a message. Maybe they weren't trying to kill us.

I could hope, at least.

"One more turn," Weston muttered.

He jerked the wheel again, this time to the left.

My body flew into the door at the sharp turn. Pain radiated up my side, and nausea churned in my stomach.

I hoped this ended well.

But I wasn't sure it would.

I CONTINUED to press my eyes closed. Continued to pray.

Everything quieted a moment.

No high chase speeds. No sudden turns. No nudges or honking horns.

At least, that's how it seemed.

Finally, after several minutes passed, I plucked my eyes open.

The road in front of us appeared normal, like nothing was amiss.

Instantly, I jerked my gaze behind me.

But I didn't see the headlights. I saw other head-lights. Normal headlights shining from a safe distance.

But I didn't see *the* headlights.

I glanced back at Weston. "Did you really lose them?"

He glanced in his rearview mirror one more time before his shoulders softened. "I made it through a stoplight. I made a few more turns, and I think I lost them."

"Did you get a good look at the car?" I gripped the door handle as my thoughts swirled, as anxiety pummeled me until I couldn't think straight.

"I tried. But it was too dark. I couldn't see anything."

I nibbled on my lip, trying to fight a frown. "That's what I figured. Why would someone be chasing us?"

"They're trying to send us a message." Weston's jaw tightened. "They're telling us to stay away. You know what that usually means, don't you?"

"What's that?" I wasn't sure I wanted to know— but I had to know.

Weston glanced at me again. "It means we must be on the right track. Somewhere with all this prodding that we've been doing, we must have struck a nerve."

I thought about everything I'd learned, but I didn't know which person I had struck a nerve with. There were still too many to name.

That meant I'd have to keep my eyes wide open.

When we got back to my apartment, Weston had been a sweetheart. He'd checked out my place to make sure it was safe before leaving me for the night.

I feared he might bring up our earlier conversation, but he didn't. I still needed more time to process what it would look like for him to leave. What that would mean for me. For us.

It wasn't fair to string him along. I needed to figure out what my intentions were.

Just as I settled on my couch to sit for a few minutes in silence, my phone rang. It was Scarlett. Instantly, my thoughts lifted.

"Hey, sweetheart," I started, my muscles relaxing ever-so-slightly. "How are you?"

"I'm great." Her voice sounded more excited than usual. "But there's something I need to tell you."

That was rarely a good thing. "What's going on?"

"I've decided to travel to Europe for the summer."

"Europe? With who?"

"Alone. I think this will be a good chance to find myself."

Any peace I'd just felt was now gone. "Alone? That sounds like a terrible idea. You need someone to watch your back, to—"

"I need to know I can do this. That I'm independent. Besides, I'll meet people along the way."

That was exactly what I feared. "It's probably too late to plan anything. Where would you stay?"

"In hostels. I don't need to plan anything. That's the beauty of it."

"Scarlett . . . you know I want you to be happy. But I don't like this. I mean, human trafficking is real and—"

"I'll be careful, Mom." Her voice held that edge of annoyance and frustration that I hated.

"Tickets are expensive—"

"I already bought mine."

I sucked in a breath. That was the next card I was going to play. Where would she get the money for it? Because I didn't plan on paying.

"How?" I asked.

"I worked at the music store both semesters and saved all my money. I used that. I even have enough left for the rest of my trip."

"Scarlett . . ." I tried to find the words to say. Tried to think of a way to convince her to stay. To maybe come live with me—which perhaps had been what I'd secretly hoped for.

"I'd love your support, Mom. I had a feeling you wouldn't love this idea."

"I don't. This is your first time traveling alone,

and it's overseas without any kind of clear itinerary. So many bad things could happen." I didn't want to think in worst-case scenarios, but how could I not? It was a scary world, and this was my daughter.

"I'll be careful," she said. "You just have to trust me."

I trusted her. I just didn't trust everyone else.

But she was nineteen and living on her own now. I wasn't sure I had much leverage.

And I remembered how I'd also encouraged her to be her own person.

But this was just one more thing to add to my list of growing worries.

CHAPTER
FOURTEEN

THE NEXT MORNING, I tried to catch up on all my projects at work. There were some things that couldn't wait, things including the summer program the conservatory was running for high schoolers. I'd written press releases about it, releases that needed to be sent out.

I'd already stopped by and talked to Jinky, and there were no updates on Annie. She was still unconscious.

Just as my lunch break started, Skittles strode into the office wearing a red top, a black skirt, and rainbow-colored knee-high socks. Her hair was in short pigtails, and her glasses today were bright blue.

But mostly I noticed the excitement lighting her gaze.

"So, I've been doing some research." She sat

across from me and leaned toward me with her elbows on the desk. "Last night, I went on some message boards for some of the more popular mukbang sites."

Now she had my attention.

I shifted back in my chair. "And?"

"*Everybody* is talking about Annie. A lot of it's nice. But you know how it goes online? The internet can bring out the nastiness in people."

Oh, yes. I knew that firsthand. "So, there were some nasty comments?"

She wagged her eyebrows up and down. "Most definitely."

"Anything of special interest?"

"There were a couple of people who were particularly hateful. People who called Annie a hack and said that she didn't deserve the fame she had anyway."

"Why would anyone say that?" I didn't want to downplay what she was doing, but it didn't seem to take a lot of special skills or talents. Or maybe I just didn't get it. Maybe there was an art to ASMR.

Skittles shrugged. "It could be any number of reasons. These people could be jealous. They could be trolls. Or they could have an honest reason why they don't like Annie—maybe even reason enough to poison her."

My assistant was learning quickly.

"Do you have any of the names?" I asked.

She pulled something from her bag and plopped it on my desk. "I printed the comments and usernames. As much as I'd like to think of myself as a computer expert, I can't trace who these people really are. That's both the beauty and the ugliness of the online world. You can be anyone you want to be—and I suspect that most of these people have fake accounts."

I took the papers from Skittles and read some of the comments. As I did, a sick feeling gurgled in my gut.

You're a hack.

Karma is telling you to quit.

Worst ASMR artist I've ever heard.

How could people be so heartless?

I didn't know, but that's definitely what these comments proved. It was just like Skittles had said.

Some people had even openly said they hoped she died.

I couldn't imagine what Annie might have done as an ASMR artist to warrant those kinds of comments.

"So, if you know anyone who's good with computers, maybe you can have them look into this. I just wanted to give you a heads-up."

"Thank you. I think I *will* have somebody look into this." This could be my best lead yet.

———

I caught a ride with Jinky to the hospital. I knew there was no change in Annie's condition, but I wanted to go anyway.

Plus, Jinky said Annie's mom, Nancy, would be there, and I hoped to ask her a few questions.

Jinky had already talked to Nancy about me coming, and I knew that it was okay.

But I wasn't prepared to see the grief on the woman's face. Seeing the tears in her eyes made everything too real for me, especially when I pictured Scarlett.

I sat down beside Nancy in the waiting room and handed her some coffee. "I thought you could use this."

She took it from me and nodded, her expression —and actions—listless. "Thank you."

Jinky lowered herself in the chair on the other side of Nancy.

The two sisters looked nothing alike. Where Jinky was boisterous and flamboyant—from the way she dressed to the way she acted—Nancy was almost mousy, with light-brown hair that hung limply, a petite build, and a soft voice.

"Any updates?" I asked.

Nancy shook her head. "I wish there were. But everything is still the same. Doctors don't even know what to tell me, but I'm really praying they don't ask me to make any gut-wrenching choices."

I knew what she meant. She was praying the hospital didn't mention having to make end-of-life decisions on whether or not to keep Annie alive.

I crossed and uncrossed my legs, trying to figure out how to compassionately find out the information I needed.

"I was hoping to ask you a few questions, if you don't mind." I kept my voice soft and not pushy.

"I want to figure out what happened to Annie, so whatever you need." She sniffled.

I pressed a tissue in her hand, hating to seem insensitive. But time wasn't on our side right now. In fact, it was working against us.

"Did Annie have any enemies?" I began.

"Not any real enemies. I mean, people could be nasty online. But Annie's pretty lovable."

"What about her ex-boyfriend, Desi?"

Nancy rolled her eyes in annoyance. "He was nothing but drama. I was so glad when the two of them broke up."

"You don't think he . . ." I couldn't finish the statement.

"He was dramatic, but he wouldn't try to hurt her," Nancy finished.

"I've heard that Annie had a different assistant before Lavern was hired," I started. "Did you know her?"

"I did, yes. Penelope. Penelope Jenkins. She and Annie had been friends for a long time."

"Do you know what happened between them?"

Nancy shrugged. "I have no idea. I kept trying to get information out of Annie, but she wouldn't share. She could overshare sometimes and be overly private at others. I guess that's just how God made her."

"Do you know how I can get up with Penelope?"

Nancy took a sip of coffee before answering. "She changed her phone number. I only know because I tried to call her to let her know what happened. Last I heard she was working at Video Game Heaven over on Eisenhower Drive."

I nodded, knowing where I needed to head next.

I glanced at Jinky and knew she was willing to go with me.

But first I wanted to let her sit with her sister another moment.

FIFTEEN

AS JINKY and I walked into Video Game Heaven, I spotted a woman behind the counter and instinctually knew she was Penelope.

The woman was short and slightly chubby with a round face and short brown hair that accentuated her round cheeks. She wore an oversized T-shirt, uncountable silver necklaces, and her pale skin was scarred with acne.

I couldn't be absolutely sure, but I may have seen her at the vigil last night.

As soon as the woman saw Jinky, her shoulders practically collapsed. She leaned against the counter as if she couldn't hold herself up. Clearly, she recognized Jinky. I assumed the two had probably met before.

She drew her gaze up to meet Jinky's as we

paused in front of her. "I heard about Annie. I'm *so* sorry."

Jinky tilted her head with grief. "We're all devastated, as you can imagine."

"I know. I've hardly gotten any sleep since I heard." Tears filled her eyes.

Penelope's sorrow looked real. I didn't get any of the same bad feelings with her as I'd gotten with Celeste. I thought she seemed sincerely sad.

"Listen, I'm Camryn, and I'm hoping you could answer some questions for me," I started.

Penelope glanced at Jinky as if to get approval.

Jinky nodded. "We've asked Camryn to look into this. She isn't an official investigator, but she's good at finding answers."

"If someone did this to Annie, then I want to find that person too. I'll answer whatever I can." She drew in a breath, seeming to straighten just slightly.

"Why did you quit working for Annie?" I dove right in rather than beating around the bush and talking platitudes.

Penelope let out a heavy sigh as if the question burdened her. "The change was all a surprise to me too, but Annie started acting really weird."

"What do you mean by really weird?" Jinky crossed her arms.

Penelope shrugged and stared at the counter—

one that had been wallpapered with various bumper stickers—a moment as if trying to gather her thoughts.

"One minute, Annie seemed like she was doing okay. Sure, Desi breaking up with her and the whole Celeste thing had her down a while. But I really thought she was looking better. One morning she came in to shoot some videos, and I could just tell something was wrong."

"Did you ask her what was going on?" I shifted and accidentally knocked a stuffed Mario on the floor. I quickly retrieved it and reminded myself to be careful.

"I did, but she said she didn't want to talk about it. Then a couple of days later, she fired me. I begged her for a reason, but she didn't give me any answers."

"Nothing happened to spur that on?" Jinky clarified.

Penelope frowned. "Nothing that I know of. It was all so strange. But as I was gathering my things, I happened to look at her desk and saw something that surprised me."

"What was it?" I asked, now totally hooked.

"It was one of those creepy notes, the ones that are made from cutting out letters in a magazine. The really old-school kind."

"What did it say?" I almost felt unable to breathe.

"It said pay fifty thousand or your secrets will be exposed."

I sucked in a breath, knowing exactly what I needed to investigate next.

"What kind of secrets?" My thoughts raced as the question left my lips.

"I have no idea." Penelope began straightening a pile of used video games in front of her. "I even asked Annie about it, and she said it was just a joke. She snatched the paper from me and tossed it in the trash. But I could tell she was trying to play it off, that she didn't mean the words. Whatever was going on had her shaken."

"You have no idea what it was?" Jinky asked.

Penelope shook her head, her hands trembling. "No, I have no idea at all. But I could tell Annie was trying to cut back on her spending. She wanted to do more low-cost shoots. I'm assuming she got over it because, even after she fired me, I watched her channel online and saw she was using the more expensive studio again."

I exchanged a look with Jinky.

Something more was definitely going on here. I needed to think through this.

I thanked Penelope and gave her my number in case she remembered anything else.

"Why would someone send Annie that note?" I asked when we were back in Jinky's car.

Jinky shook her head. "I have no idea. It doesn't make any sense. Annie is a good girl. She never got herself wrapped up in any trouble that I know of. If she did, I bet it was all Desi's fault."

"She and Desi were broken up by then, weren't they?"

Her gaze narrowed. "They were. But I still wouldn't put it past him to cause trouble for her. The fact he's missing right now only confirms those thoughts."

I couldn't deny what she said. Desi's disappearance *did* seem suspicious.

Fighting a headache, I leaned back in the car seat.

Instead of finding more answers, I felt like I was only finding more questions.

I didn't know how to fix that.

And that was a problem—especially since I was supposed to be a fixer.

CHAPTER
SIXTEEN

WHEN WE GOT BACK to the conservatory, I worked for a couple of hours.

Then I decided to take a walk.

To the police station.

The nearest precinct was a considerable distance away, but I didn't want to ask anyone for another ride, nor did I want to call Uber. Besides, walking helped clear my head.

I didn't come up with any solutions as I placed one foot in front of the other. But I did review everything I'd learned.

Then I reviewed the current situation with Weston. Scarlett. My dad.

So much was going on.

I kept thinking that as I got older life would be

easier. But that never seemed to be the case. If anything, it was simply more complicated.

When I got to the station, I asked for Detective Garrison at the front desk. To my surprise, he agreed to see me right away. I was escorted to his desk by a uniformed officer.

Garrison leaned back in his chair as he observed me. "I wondered how long it would take for you to show up here again."

Without invitation, I lowered myself into the chair across from him. I sat stiffly, not wanting to get too comfortable. "I've been looking into what happened to Annie."

He nodded slowly. "I figured you would, especially considering your connection to the crime. How is Annie doing?"

"The same."

He nodded slowly again. "That was the last that I heard also."

"I know that you think Lavern did this." I tried to broach the subject carefully—but that was really what I needed to talk to him about.

"She has the motive, means, and opportunity."

I twisted my head. "Are you sure about that?"

His jaw flicked with tension before relaxing again. "The motive would be to start her own channel and eliminate the competition. She clearly had the means to substitute a blue-ringed octopus for a regular octopus, and she also had the opportunity to pull off the switch since she was Annie's assistant."

That sounded okay on paper, but in reality, it didn't make sense. "I looked up these octopuses . . . octopi . . . whatever. Anyway . . . the blue-ringed octopus has a distinct appearance. It would have been obvious it wasn't a normal one."

"People have been known to bleach them. Did you know that was possible?"

I blinked. "I didn't know that. But let's say that's what happened. Where would Lavern even get this octopus?"

"You'd be surprised what kind of things people deal—things other than drugs. Where there's a will, there's a way. We're checking all her purchases. Believe me."

I swallowed hard, knowing I needed to change tactics. "Did you know that Annie was being threatened? I'm not talking about the notes she told you about. It went further than that. Someone anonymous insisted she give them money or that her secrets would be exposed."

The way Garrison's eyes flickered made me think he hadn't heard that before even though he didn't say that. "Where did you hear that?"

I shrugged. "I've been asking a lot of questions.

Her former assistant mentioned it to me. She found the note on Annie's desk."

"And you didn't think to report that to the police?"

He had a good point. "I just found out today, and it's hearsay. But you're right—I should have mentioned it right away. My apologies."

His gaze narrowed as if he wasn't sure if he'd accept my apology or not. "What else did you hear?"

I had nothing to gain by keeping any information from him. If anything, Garrison could take what I told him and use it to find answers. That's what I hoped at least.

I had no reason to doubt the detective's abilities. He'd only been upright in the past, and I hoped he continued to be that way.

For that reason, I filled him in on everything I'd learned.

"I only want to find out what truly happened," I concluded. "I know you think that the answers are obvious. But I'm not sure that I agree."

His expression didn't make it clear if he was on the same page as me or not. "I'll look into this extortion threat and see what I can figure out."

I shifted in my seat. "I'm sure you already knew Annie was in some debt."

He remained quiet before saying, "I was

surprised that, considering the amount of money she made, she had nothing in her bank account and her credit cards were maxed."

That only confirmed what Lavern had told me about the credit card being declined when she'd gone to pick up the seafood.

"Does that mean she actually paid off whoever had threatened her?" I asked.

He shrugged. "Hard to say, but that sounds like a good guess. Maybe that's why Annie seemed pretty relaxed recently. Maybe she thought her problems were over."

I leaned back, questions still peppering me. "What I can't figure out is *why*. Why would anyone threaten her? What do they have to hold over her?"

Garrison let out a breath. "That's something we're going to need to look into."

As we were talking, Garrison's phone beeped. The detective narrowed his eyes before putting the device to his ear. "What's up?"

I listened closely, able to make out what was being said on the other line. I really tried not to eavesdrop most of the time. But right now, I wanted to gather all the information I could.

I could very clearly hear what was being said on both sides of this phone conversation.

Garrison was talking to someone at the lab.

The octopus Annie had eaten was *not* poisonous.

Instead, Annie had ingested rat poison . . . a substance that had been found in the coating of her fried chicken.

I didn't tell Detective Garrison I'd overheard his conversation. Instead, I stored the information away to address later.

Although I *did* wonder if Garrison knew I'd overheard something. His leery expression indicated that might be the case.

I didn't ask. It was better if I didn't know—probably the same for him.

Instead, I started walking back to the college when I heard a footfall behind me.

I glanced over my shoulder, but I didn't see anyone in particular—only throngs of people from a local jazz festival taking place down at the waterfront. They must have bled over to this area on a break between acts or something.

But I didn't see anyone who looked especially suspicious.

I took several more steps. Matching footsteps continued to sound behind me.

When I glanced over my shoulder, I again saw no one.

But I was nearly certain that I was being followed.

My heart thumped harder.

I remembered what Weston had said last night—that the closer I got to finding answers, the more someone might feel pressured to stop me from looking.

Was that what was happening right now?

CHAPTER
SEVENTEEN

I MADE it safely back to my apartment.

But I knew I needed to address the situation with my dad. He was still at Weston's, and I couldn't simply expect Weston to take care of my father for me—even if he *had* volunteered.

So, after I freshened up, I caught an Uber to Weston's.

As usual, Weston's eyes lit up when he answered the door and saw me.

I *loved* it when he looked at me like that—I loved it more than I should.

I had to face the facts—another heartbreak by Weston might destroy me the second time around.

I mentally paused.

Actually, it wouldn't. I was a much stronger person now than I'd been back in my early twenties.

Having my heart broken wouldn't be fun, but it wouldn't crush me.

I would pull through and move on—just as I had every heartbreak and trauma I'd experienced.

"I was just going to call you." Weston's voice snapped me from my thoughts.

He leaned in the doorway and grinned lazily as if he had all the time in the world.

I'd like more than anything to simply stand here and admire that look. But it wasn't an option—not considering everything that had happened and the task I'd come here to accomplish.

"It's good to see you," I said instead. "But I really felt like I needed to check on my father."

His lips flickered down in what looked like disappointment. He quickly recovered and said, "He just got back."

My eyebrows shot up. "Just got back where? Here?"

Weston nodded and moved aside to let me in. He was going to let my father explain for himself.

Smart move.

I found my father in the living room. He was grinning as if the past ten years had been erased and none of his crimes had happened.

"What's been going on?" I paused in front of him, waiting for his explanation and wondering again where he'd gotten more new clothes. I didn't bother to sit. Standing helped me feel more in control.

"I just got back from the city." Dad's voice sounded rich and warm. "I love how walkable Savannah is. I can get to anywhere I want to go. There's great scenery. Great food. Great people."

"Where are you getting money to buy new clothes, Dad?" I decided to ask him point-blank about his outfits.

His gaze remained bright. "I had some money tucked away just in case I needed it. I'm also working on getting a new place to stay. With any luck, I should be able to move in by tomorrow."

I tried not to gape. "A new place? Where in the world would you have money to get a new place?"

"Like I said, I have some cash tucked away."

"How is that even possible?" My voice rose, though I willed myself to remain calm. "All your assets were seized to pay back your victims. There's no way you have money *tucked away*."

His smile slipped a little.

He didn't like the fact I was questioning him instead of simply accepting what he had to say. That was what most people did. Dad was just so convincing, and people wanted to believe him, wanted to champion his ideas. His personality was his best asset.

He cleared his throat. "Authorities could only take money from me that they knew about. I *may* have hidden some cash and put it away for a rainy day, just in case."

I twisted my head. "Dad, I don't want to see you get in trouble again."

"Don't worry your pretty head about it." He shrugged. "I'll be out of your hair soon."

"But—"

"You always worry about me so much." He let out a slow chuckle, but I had trouble believing he felt as assured as he acted. "But I'm taking care of things just fine. I'm grateful Weston has let me stay here a couple of days."

"You didn't take anything of his, did you?" I didn't want to ask the question, but I had to. I had to know.

"Camryn . . ." Weston's voice held an edge of caution, as if he tried to warn me not to do something I might regret.

"It's okay." My father's smile disappeared completely. "No, I didn't take anything of Weston's. I promise you."

I stared at my dad another moment, trying to figure out if he was telling the truth or not.

At this point, I had no choice but to trust him.

But trusting him was the last thing that I wanted

to do.

Because in the past he'd only let me down.

Before I'd left Weston's last night, I'd grabbed a few minutes alone with him so I could whisper some thoughts.

Yes, whisper.

I knew my theory probably sounded crazy, but I'd always secretly wondered if my dad also had unique hearing abilities and if he'd utilized them as a part of his cons in the past.

That was why I'd whispered to Weston outside the door—just in case. I'd told him the lab had found rat poison in the chicken batter and that Annie hadn't eaten a poisonous octopus.

And that changed the whole case.

I had to assume it would be difficult to narrow down where the rat poison had come from. Then again, maybe it didn't matter as much where the poisoning had come from as it did how the substance had gotten in the batter for the fried chicken.

As far as I knew, the only people who'd handled those ingredients were Annie and Lavern. I had a hard time thinking Annie had done this to herself.

I needed to see if anyone else had gotten close to

the food—anyone I hadn't seen at the studio. I had arrived after Annie already started filming, after all.

The only person I knew to talk to about that was Lavern.

I took an Uber to her house before work. I knew I was probably showing up too early, but I had to make the most of my time.

And it didn't matter. Because when I arrived, the police were already there. I figured they would have come last night, but maybe it had taken a while to get a search warrant. Maybe they were backed up with other cases. Or maybe they'd come last night, *and* they'd come back again today to look for something else.

I asked the Uber driver to wait for me as I stepped onto a small patch of lawn in front of the building.

No sooner had I done that did Detective Garrison step out.

He didn't look entirely surprised to see me.

He paused in front of me, his hands going to his hips as his shaded gaze met mine. "Did Lavern call you?"

I shook my head, surprised by the sharpness in his tone. "No. Why? What's going on?"

"Don't play dumb, Camryn. I know you overheard that phone conversation yesterday. You know about the rat poison."

I didn't deny it. "So . . . ?"

I left the question open-ended, an invitation for Garrison to share more if he felt he could.

He pressed his lips together before saying, "There was rat poison inside Lavern's apartment. Underneath the sink."

I sucked in a breath, even though I didn't find that fact all that surprising. A lot of people had rat poison in their homes. "That's still circumstantial."

"Maybe." His gaze remained unchanged. "But it's another piece of evidence that could prove Lavern is the one behind this."

"I really don't think she's the one who did this, and I'm determined to figure out who is really responsible." I meant the words. I didn't care how the evidence was stacking up. I just couldn't see Lavern as the one who poisoned Annie.

He grunted and took a step back. "Good luck with that."

I glanced behind him at the battered old apartment building. "Is Lavern still inside?"

"She is. But if you're wanting to talk to her, I'm not sure how much she'll be willing to say. She's pretty upset."

I nodded, knowing I needed to take my chances.

But first, I needed to tell my Uber driver he could leave. I had a feeling I would be here for a while.

CHAPTER
EIGHTEEN

I'D ALREADY BEEN SITTING with Lavern for fifteen minutes, trying to comfort her. Her mom wasn't a lot of help. In fact, I wondered if Julie was taking some type of anti-anxiety medicine. Her eyes looked glazed and her movements subdued.

She'd only perked up when she'd decided to get a manicure and had made the appointment.

"Who else could've had contact with the food?" I asked.

"No one else had contact with the food." Lavern leaned forward, her face in her hands as unseen burdens wedged on her shoulders. "Annie and I went shopping together, but I kept the groceries in my car. When we got to the studio, I pulled every-thing out and set up. Annie's the one who cooked. It doesn't make any sense how anyone else would have had a chance to poison anything."

"Did you guys stop anywhere on the way to the studio after you picked up the groceries?"

Lavern shrugged as she shook her head, acting as if the question exhausted her.

"I really need for you to think this through," I told her. "Can you start from the beginning and be more specific?"

She drew in a deep breath before releasing it as if trying to gather herself.

"We stopped by Food Express first," she finally said. "We were probably inside twenty minutes and never left the cart unattended. I put everything in the back of my car and then we stopped at The Oriental Grocer to get the octopus. After that, we went straight to the studio."

"Did you and Annie both get out of the car at The Oriental Grocer?"

"We did. Why? Do you think someone snuck the poisoning into the flour while we went inside?" She froze, almost as if she wasn't going to breathe until I answered.

"Well, if you didn't do it, and Haruto didn't do it, then we need to look for an opportunity where someone else *could* do it."

It sounded so hard to believe. But, if Lavern was innocent, then it was the only thing that made sense.

"Could you tell if anything had been tampered with?"

"Now that you mention it, Annie brought the flour from her house, as well as the sugar and a few eggs. I *guess* those things could've been tampered with before she brought them with her." She shrugged as if unconvinced.

I nodded and rose. "That's all I need to know. Thank you."

Lavern stared at me with her red-rimmed eyes. "Do you think you can do something with that information?"

I sighed. "I can't say for sure, but I'm going to do my best to prove your innocence. You have my word."

Instead of calling an Uber, I called Jinky.

I wanted to see inside Annie's apartment myself. I wanted to look at her kitchen. Maybe talk to a neighbor.

I didn't know. But her place seemed like the next logical area to look.

Jinky picked me up, and we went there. Nancy was staying at Jinky's place, so no one was home when we stepped inside. Annie didn't have a roommate, which would make this all even more complicated.

"You really think you're going to find something here?" Jinky paused in the doorway, a fresh round of grief on her face.

Coming here was difficult. I knew it would be. But I appreciated her doing this for me.

"I don't know," I told her. "It's hard to say. But it's worth a look at least, right?"

Jinky nodded, her actions more subdued than usual. "Right. Do you want me to help you look?"

"If you wouldn't mind looking for rat poison, that would be great."

She froze. "Do you think she put the rat poison in her own food? That would be a crazy way of getting ratings."

"No, I don't think Annie added it herself." I opened a closet next to the kitchen and found cleaning supplies. "Could it have been an accident maybe? Did Annie get it mixed up? From what I know about Annie, she's too smart to do that. But I'm just trying to examine every angle—just as the police will."

"Your thoroughness is appreciated." Jinky

seemed to snap out of her daze. "I'll see what I can find."

I found nothing in the cleaning closet, so I began going through the kitchen cabinets.

There was a surprising lack of food here at Annie's place. I assumed that someone who did what she did for a living would have all kinds of food experiments going on.

But that's not what I saw.

Jinky and I searched the whole kitchen before pausing.

We had found nothing.

Which took me back to my original theory that maybe someone had tampered with that flour when they went to The Oriental Grocer.

I could go back there and talk to Haruto and ask if he had any cameras outside. It seemed worth a shot.

But before I left Annie's place, there were still a few more things that I wanted to check out.

CHAPTER
NINETEEN

I HESITATED before going into Annie's room.

Her space felt too personal.

But I knew searching it was a necessary evil.

Had the police already been inside? I assumed, if they were being thorough, that they had.

Carefully, I walked the perimeter, soaking everything in before touching things.

Her room seemed surprisingly subdued considering Annie's personality. Everything was white and gray, from the bedspread to the rug. Her dresser was clear with no clothes scattered on top. A picture of Annie, Jinky, and Nancy stood on the nightstand.

Then there was her desk. Also neat.

And also the best place to find answers.

I lowered myself into the chair there and sucked in several deep breaths before opening the drawers.

Nothing out of the ordinary was inside the first drawer. Just your standard office supplies—a stapler, some paper clips, and notepads. But nothing exciting.

I moved on to her next drawer, which just contained bills—electric, water, insurance.

They didn't really tell me anything either.

But when I opened the third drawer and moved aside several file folders, something finally caught my eye. Something that had been shoved between some scripts and ideas for upcoming shows.

Something that looked like a contract.

I pulled it closer so I could read the words.

According to the date on the first page, this was an endorsement deal Annie had been offered only three days ago. It appeared to be with a national restaurant chain called Pickard's Poultry—an establishment known for their fried chicken.

The chain wanted Annie to come up with a special, limited-edition recipe for them to feature on their menus. In exchange for creating the recipe and advertising it on her channel, Pickard's would pay her a substantial amount.

I quickly scanned the text before my eyes widened.

If Annie signed this deal, she would receive half a million dollars.

That kind of money could change her life.

I was surprised no one had brought this endorsement deal up yet.

Unless they didn't know.

Had the police seen this? It seemed as if they might have gone through her desk, just in case. But this had been mixed in with some other paperwork. They could have skimmed right by it.

I sucked on my bottom lip in thought.

After contemplating my next step a moment, I grabbed my phone and quickly took pictures of the contract, including the cover letter which had the name of Annie's contact at corporate—someone named Brenda Verbanski.

I slipped the contract back into the drawer so it could be ready for Annie when she woke up.

Because I had to believe she was going to wake up.

Any other option wasn't okay.

"An endorsement deal for half a million dollars?" Jinky repeated as we climbed into her car.

I nodded. "That's what the paperwork said."

Jinky shook her head as she stared into the

distance in shock. "Why wouldn't Annie have told me something about that? I thought we shared everything. I mean, we try to get together for dinner twice a week. She calls me at night before she goes to bed. We're tight."

I shrugged, knowing nothing I said would make her feel better. "I have no idea. But I wonder if someone else was in the running for that endorsement deal. That would be a great motive for murder."

"I still can't believe this." Jinky shook her head as we sat in her car, doors open to let a soft breeze inside. "I can't believe someone would plot to hurt my precious niece. I hope she's okay."

A tear trickled down her cheek. I knew her emotions had been building up all morning, and I felt terrible for her. Seeing loved ones suffer was never easy. In fact, it was one of the worst things of all.

I pulled my friend into a quick hug, her coarse blonde hair tickling my cheek and her pungent perfume taking my breath away. But I didn't care. I only wanted my friend to feel better, to know she wasn't alone.

"I want Annie to be okay also," I whispered. "I'm praying for her every day."

As I pulled back, Jinky's gaze caught mine, and I saw the questions in her eyes.

"How are you going to find out more about this endorsement?" she asked.

I leaned back in my seat and thought about the question a moment. "I'm not 100 percent sure. But there's a name and number listed on this contract. I thought I'd call to see if I can find out more information, even though I'm not sure how much this person is going to tell me."

"It seems like a good place to start." She glanced at me. "I'm glad we're having dinner together tonight. That's still on, isn't it? I could use the distraction."

That was right. Weston and I were supposed to eat with Jinky and her new boyfriend this evening. We'd planned it last week, but with all the craziness going on, I'd forgotten.

"Yes, definitely. I think Weston made the reservation."

"Great." But her excitement lasted only a minute. Then she stared out the window again and frowned. "I just wish Annie would wake up. If she could talk to us, then maybe she could give us some insight . . ." Her voice faded wistfully.

I squeezed her arm. I hoped that was the case also. I wanted this all to be over and for everyone to have a happy ending . . . right after the person who had hurt Annie was arrested.

But right now, I needed to get to the office.

I had some work to do for the conservatory.

Then I wanted to give Brenda Verbanski a call.

CHAPTER
TWENTY

AS SOON AS I saw Skittles, I knew something was up—even before I said a word to her about the endorsement deal.

She sat at her desk, looking at her computer with wide, curious eyes. Her eyes never got wide like that when she was simply working.

That probably meant she was scrolling the internet and had stumbled upon something juicy.

"Did you hear?" She looked up at me, her eyes still like saucers.

My heart slowed as I thought about Annie. I'd just been with Jinky, and she would have been one of the first people to know if something had happened to Annie.

So clearly, I didn't know.

"What's going on?" I moved closer.

She turned her computer screen toward me. "Maybe it's better if you watch."

Another ASMR artist filled the screen. I thought I'd seen a couple of her videos when I was doing my research. Krissy Stovall was the name listed at the bottom in big block letters—as if she didn't want anyone to have any confusion about who she was.

My throat tightened as I watched, as I anticipated what was about to happen.

The woman in the video, who couldn't be any more than twenty-two years old, lifted a shrimp with her chopsticks and popped it in her mouth. The sound of her chewing filled the speakers and, as to be expected, made me squirm.

But I tried to focus on everything else instead. Everything besides the sounds.

I really hoped Skittles was going somewhere with this by showing me this video. Because right now, I was just watching this woman eat her food and all the neurons in my brain were rebelling.

A moment later, Krissy froze. Her hands went to her throat. Her eyes widened as she stared at the camera, her gaze clearly trying to communicate something.

Then she stood and began coughing.

As if she was choking.

The camera tilted slightly as if someone had hit it.

A man appeared on the screen, patting the woman's back.

But the motion didn't help.

Krissy collapsed to the floor and out of sight.

Several seconds later, the feed ended.

My heart beat rapidly as I comprehended what I had just seen.

I glanced at Skittles. "When was this posted?"

"Apparently, Krissy was doing this show live when this happened. That was an hour ago."

My heart pounded harder. "Have you heard any updates since then?"

Skittles frowned. "Nothing official, but it's all over the internet that she died. Do you think the same person who tried to target Annie also targeted this woman?"

My throat tightened.

I didn't know.

But the theory made a lot of sense.

Back in the privacy of my office, I called Detective Garrison. I figured he already knew about this other YouTuber, but just in case he didn't . . .

He answered right away, and I shared the update with him.

He sounded genuinely surprised when he asked, "What? What's her name?"

I rattled it off.

"I'll look into it," Garrison said. "Do you know where she lives?"

"My assistant thinks she lives in Florida, so not terribly far away."

"I appreciate you sharing that with me. Thank you."

Before he got off the call, I also told him about the contract I'd found. I figured he needed to know. Again, he sounded surprised.

Maybe he wasn't as competent as I was giving him credit for . . .

As soon as I ended that call, I thought about Lavern. I'd seen her this morning. So, there was no way she could be responsible for this . . . right? Or was Detective Garrison crazy enough to think she'd left in the middle of the night and driven to Florida to somehow taint this girl's food before driving back?

That would be a stretch, right?

At least, I hoped that was the case.

Had Krissy actually died because she'd choked on the shrimp? Or had she also been poisoned?

I hated the thought of it, but the theory was one I needed to explore.

I found the video on my own computer and watched it again.

Before Krissy had eaten that shrimp, she'd also had pancakes, a hamburger, and french fries.

I didn't know how these women stayed so thin eating so much, but good for them.

Poison could have been added to any of that food, but pancakes seemed the most likely.

I had to stop thinking about it. I was sure investigators in Florida would be looking into the matter.

For now, I needed to sit back and let them do their job.

Instead, I pulled out my phone and glanced at the images I'd taken of that endorsement deal.

Brenda Verbanski.

Should I call her?

Maybe.

But first, I had another thought I wanted to explore, a theory I wanted to test.

I found Krissy Stovall's channel and searched all her videos.

I needed to know if fried chicken was one of her hallmark foods as well.

Because that would have made her a direct competitor of Annie's.

I didn't have to search many videos before I found the ones I was looking for.

Yes, Krissy Stovall also loved fried chicken—Pickard's Poultry, to be exact.

There was no way that was a coincidence.

SEATED AT MY DESK STILL, I dialed the number from the contract and asked for Brenda Verbanski. She answered on the second ring.

Now, I hoped she'd actually talk to me.

I told her who I was and why I'd called, but then she had to put me on hold for a few minutes. I was beginning to think she wasn't coming back when she finally did.

"Who are you again?" Brenda asked, even though I'd already explained myself. Her voice sounded brisk and narrow with professionalism.

"I'm Camryn Paine, and I'm investigating the supposed murder attempt on Annie King."

"Yes, I was so sorry to hear about that." Her voice softened. "All of us here at Pickard's Poultry are rooting for her to pull through. But I'm not sure why you're calling me."

"I found the endorsement deal offer, and I can't help but wonder if that has something to do with what happened to Annie—or maybe even Krissy Stovall."

A brief pause sounded. "What do you mean?"

"I mean, that kind of money is something people would go to extremes for. I wondered if there were other YouTubers in the running for that deal."

She let out a short, almost condescending chuckle. "I can't tell you that."

I figured she'd say as much. "Certainly, other people could have gotten this deal, but you chose Annie."

"This is what I can tell you. We liked her brand. We liked that she was a local girl—we're based out of Charleston. The board thought she would be a good fit. It took a lot of convincing for corporate to decide to even want to try this new marketing tactic. Using social media stars in advertisements is something foreign to some of the old-timers around here."

"I understand." It was slightly foreign to me also, but I'd done a quick search and saw that other chains —even Taco Bell and Dunkin'—had done similar things. "Can you answer this at least? Was Annie going to take the deal?"

"I talked to her several times, and she sounded like she was going to. She seemed very excited, for that matter. I'm sure the money she was going to receive helped her make up her mind."

I frowned as I chewed on that thought. "It's odd. None of Annie's friends and family seemed to know anything about it."

"It's in the contract that she's not supposed to tell anybody—except legal counsel—until it's signed. We like to keep this top secret, just in case . . ."

"Just in case what?" I had a feeling she was going somewhere with this—somewhere I might not like.

"These kinds of deals can be cutthroat." Brenda's voice turned crispy again. "That's all I can tell you. Now, I really must get back to work."

Before I could ask any more questions, the line went dead.

I tried to make the rest of my workday productive by knocking several things off my to-do list.

But my mind stayed on Annie King and what had happened to her.

There were still several things I needed to follow up on.

One was Haruto. I called him and was surprised

when he answered. However, he said he didn't have any security cameras out front. That lead died quickly.

The next thing I wanted to follow up on was the nasty comments made online about Annie.

My husband, Phil, had owned a private security firm that my brother, Joel, now ran. If my memory served me correctly, the firm had a computer expert on staff.

His name was Dave Kimball. I decided to give him a call.

"Camryn . . . it's been a long time," Dave said. "How's it going?"

"Life goes on," I said.

It was one of my standard lines. But my words were true. No matter what happened, good or bad, time marched on and waited for no one. The older I got, the more I realized that was true.

"I'm assuming you're calling for another reason other than catching up . . ." Dave said.

"I am." I explained to him that I was looking into what happened to Annie King and the horrible messages left online for her. "Is there any way you can trace who sent those messages?"

He made a long, uncertain mumbling sound. "It's complicated. I can probably track down the IP address and give you a basic location. Maybe, if I search deep enough, I could even tell you who the computer was registered to. It's all still speculation at that point."

"I understand. I'm just trying to see if there are any overlapping names if that makes sense."

"It makes perfect sense. Why don't you go ahead and send me the link to some of those comments and I'll see what I can find out."

"That sounds perfect. Thank you so much. I'll do that as soon as I get off the phone."

And I did. As soon as I ended the call, I found the information I was looking for and sent it to him.

Then I just had to wait to see what Dave would find out.

TWENTY-TWO

JINKY, her boyfriend Jeff, Weston, and I were all supposed to go to dinner together tonight.

Doing so seemed so mundane considering all that had happened. But I knew it would be good for all of us to get out and clear our heads.

Plus, I wanted to get to know Jinky's new boyfriend a little better.

We'd chosen a casual restaurant. Gloria's was located in downtown Savannah in the historic district. It required reservations, which was fine by me since I didn't have time to waste waiting for a table.

Jinky and Jeff were already seated by the time Weston and I arrived. The two of us had met outside the restaurant—Weston had a late class today—so we hadn't had any time to catch up. I'd wanted to fill him in on the day, but I hadn't had the opportunity to do so yet.

I tried to steal a few moments as we followed the hostess toward our table.

"Things have gotten crazy," I whispered to Weston. As I leaned closer to him, I caught a whiff of his cologne.

The scent made me want to lean into him more, to relish the leathery aroma.

Instead, I eased back, trying to control my thoughts.

"Crazy with the investigation or crazy because more trouble has found you?" Weston turned toward me, his face entirely too close.

But I wasn't complaining.

My heart was still pitter-pattering as I said, "Thankfully, it's just with the investigation. Speaking of which . . . did you hear about Krissy Stovall?"

There was nothing like a murder to splash cold water on any hot feelings.

Weston took my elbow as we maneuvered between the tables. "I heard something about it on the news. I almost called you to tell you."

"What if the same person is responsible for both Annie and Krissy's incidents?"

Weston tilted his head skeptically. "Considering the fact that Krissy lived in Florida . . ."

"I know. It's a stretch. But Jacksonville is less than three hours from here."

"That's true. Hopefully, the police are looking into it."

Just as we reached our table, my gaze traveled across the restaurant.

I stopped on one person. Actually, two.

It was my father.

He was having dinner with Julie, Lavern's mom.

The air left my lungs when I saw them.

But my shock only lasted a moment.

The emotion quickly morphed into anger. What kind of stunt was my dad trying to pull now?

I switched direction and charged across the restaurant toward them, determined to find out some answers.

"What do you think you're doing?" I demanded as I paused by my father's table and jammed my hands onto my hips.

Weston appeared behind me, but he didn't shush me. Instead, he simply seemed to be there for support.

My dad's eyes widened, and he stiffened when he saw me. "Camryn?"

"Aren't you Annie's friend?" Julie said at the same time, tilting her head as she studied me.

The woman was dressed to the nines, as the saying went, wearing a form-fitting black dress and heels. Her hair was swept up in a twist that accentuated the unique angles of her face.

Even though the woman had a daughter in her early twenties, Julie could easily pass as someone in her mid-thirties.

"What are you two doing here?" I ignored the questioning looks of everyone around me. I needed answers.

"I'm just having dinner with my new friend here." My dad flashed a smile. "Is there anything wrong with that?"

To anyone who might be listening, my dad might sound casual. But I heard the edge in his voice. He was trying to keep me quiet.

"How did the two of you even meet?" I demanded.

I knew I might sound like a brat, but I was done playing games here.

"I was on a morning walk when we ran into each other and began to talk," Julie said. "We hit it off, and it was a nice distraction from the nightmare that's become my life. Sure, I feel a little guilty going out to dinner after everything that's happened but . . .

Lavern said it would be good for me. She gave me her blessing."

I swerved my gaze back to my father. "Dad?"

"It's just like Julie said," he started. "We ran into each other, and now here we are enjoying each other's company. There's nothing wrong with that."

"Dad . . ." Warning sounded in my voice. I wasn't buying this. Not for one minute.

The world might be small, but it wasn't that small.

"Yes?" He glanced up at me, his voice restrained.

"Can I talk to you outside for a moment?"

He shifted his gaze before smiling. "Of course, you can, sweet pea." He glanced at Julie. "Excuse me for a moment."

With that, he rose from his seat.

It took every ounce of my self-control to not spill every negative thought in my mind as we walked toward the exit.

I TOLD Weston he could wait inside. This conversation was best left private between my father and me.

As soon as we were outside and had stepped around the corner, I let my father have it.

I crossed my arms as I stared at him. "Are you trying to con Julie?"

"Of course not. Why would you say that?" Dad had the nerve to look offended.

"Because that's what you do."

"I'm a changed man. I told you." He raised his chin defiantly.

"You're going to have to prove that before I believe it."

"Sweet pea . . ." He started to reach for me, but I

jerked back. "I'm sorry I've broken your trust. I can see I have some work to do."

I wasn't buying his act. My gaze remained locked with his. "Did you know who Julie was before you asked her to dinner?"

Something flickered in his gaze. "It seems like the two of you may have met. But I didn't know that."

"Are you sure about that? Or did you get curious about what I was investigating and start snooping? In the process, did you discover the Blackmores were wealthy and that Julie was single?"

"I wouldn't do that." But right before he said those words, I heard the saliva swishing in his mouth —a sure sign he was contemplating his words a little too much.

More anger rose inside me, and I pulled my arms more tightly over my chest. "What's your game? What are you trying to get out of Julie? More money?"

"We're just having dinner, Camryn." His voice turned harder, as if he was done trying to be nice. "You can't make me feel guilty about that. I've been locked up for a long time. I've been lonely."

"You were locked up because you conned people out of millions of dollars. And now you're back out on the streets again."

"I didn't hurt anyone." His voice hardened again. "Sure, I took their money. But I wasn't dangerous. I didn't deserve to spend the rest of my life in prison."

"I'm sure there are a lot of people who would beg to differ."

"Camryn . . ."

I started to step back toward the restaurant, done with this conversation. But, instead, I paused and turned toward my father as I realized I still had more to say. "I don't want you seeing her again, Dad. Do you understand? And you need to be out of Weston's house ASAP."

My dad stared at me another moment, something close to hurt in his gaze. But I could never trust his eyes. He could manipulate his features like an artist could manipulate paint.

"Understood," he finally said.

Then I stormed back into the restaurant, determined to enjoy myself.

Enjoying myself wasn't working out.

When I went into the restaurant, I saw that three women had surrounded the table harassing Weston for autographs.

Actually, harassing wasn't the right word. They were being friendly. But it was also causing a scene, and my stress levels were messing with my brain.

Between them and the confrontation I'd just had with my father, I knew the rest of the evening was on the rocks.

I glanced at Jinky, and I could tell she knew what I was thinking.

"I think we should cut our losses and grab something to eat somewhere else," I said.

I reached into my wallet, pulled out some cash, and left it on the table to pay for our sudden departure.

Even if it wasn't for all the drama, I knew I didn't want to sit here and watch my father have dinner with Julie.

After signing some napkins, Weston excused himself from the women and then we strolled outside.

I could tell by the look in his eyes that he was concerned about me. He placed a hand on my back and gently rubbed it as the four of us stood on the sidewalk.

"Everything around here has to be booked." I sighed as I glanced around. There were plenty of restaurants in the area, but it was dinnertime and this part of town was popular.

"How about over there?" Weston pointed across the street.

"Burger Queen?" I wasn't sure I'd heard him correctly.

"Every once in a while, I get a hankering for one of their Stack Attacks," Weston said.

"Me too," Jinky added, raising her eyebrows as if she liked the idea.

Jeff shrugged. "I'm always up for whatever."

I was thankful to have friends who were so accommodating. "Burger Queen it is then."

We had to take a couple of crosswalks and dodge some traffic, but we finally made our way inside and ordered.

Then we found a booth in the back and sat down with our burgers, fries, and sodas.

I bit into my burger, which was surprisingly good.

"I'm curious—what did your dad say?" Jinky asked as she dabbed a fry into a tiny paper bucket of ketchup. "Your conversation looked intense."

I knew everyone wanted to know. And I didn't mind sharing with Weston and Jinky. I didn't know Jeff that well. Even though he seemed nice enough, I knew I still needed to be careful. Privacy was a trea-sure—a lesson I'd learned after being exploited in the limelight.

"He claims it's all a coincidence that they met," I said. "But I don't trust him. I feel like he has ulterior motives."

"It can't be a coincidence that he's going out with Julie . . ." Weston said.

"That's what I think too. I'm assuming he knows that Lavern's mom has money." I looked at Jinky for confirmation.

"Annie didn't talk a lot about Lavern's family," Jinky offered before taking a quick sip of her soda. "But I had the impression Lavern was trying to get away from all of that. That she didn't like being tied to her family's money and that's why she wanted to strike out on her own."

"Do you know anything else about her family? What her parents do for a living?" I was only asking because I was trying to figure out more of what my dad might be thinking.

"Her dad died a few years ago of a heart attack, but he worked in finance." Jinky waved a fry in the air. "He was very successful, apparently."

My mind raced through my dad's last scheme, the one that had landed him in prison.

The one where he had sold property he didn't own.

Frustration continued to churn inside me.

I had enough going on without adding my father's schemes into an already long list.

But it looked like I didn't have any choice except to deal with this situation head-on.

TWENTY-FOUR

I HAD to admit that the evening turned out better than I thought it would.

Being with my friends had turned my cranky mood into something more acceptable, and I actually found myself loosening up.

Plus, I surprisingly enjoyed my burger and fries. Afterward, the four of us had splurged and had walked to a little ice cream shop down the road. At Christmastime, they had gingerbread ice cream, which was amazing. Today, I settled for Rocky Road.

After we finished, we said goodbye to Jinky and Jeff, and then walked toward Weston's truck. But right when we reached it, Weston grabbed my arm to stop me from climbing inside. His imploring gaze met mine. "Are you okay?"

The sincerity in his voice nearly left me feeling undone.

I pushed a hair behind my ear and nodded. "I think. Maybe not. I don't really know."

The more I talked, the more my conviction seemed to crumble.

"I'm sorry, Camryn." He reached for me and pulled me into a long hug.

I nestled my head beneath his chin, relaxing in his embrace. I couldn't seem to refuse the comfort he offered.

I thought I was doing okay since Phil passed, but there were things I missed. Companionship. Having somebody there to lift me when I fell.

All those emotions came rushing back to me now.

Then I remembered that Weston could be leaving. He might say that it was just for the summer. But what if it wasn't? I hated to always think in worst-case scenarios, but I had to act like an adult here.

I stepped back and tried to compose myself as our gazes met again.

"Thank you," I muttered. But my voice cracked and gave away some of the emotions that were simmering inside me.

The look in Weston's eyes was pure affection as he studied me. He reached toward me and pushed a hair out of my face. He lingered close, and the moment felt intimate.

I swallowed hard, realizing that more than anything I just wanted to reach up and skim my fingers across his face. His beard.

I wanted to lean close again and get another whiff of his clean but leathery cologne.

I wanted to pick up where the two of us had left off more than twenty years ago.

But I just didn't know if I could let go enough to actually do that.

My phone buzzed, drawing me out of the moment.

Which could be a good thing.

I muttered an apology as I pulled the phone out and checked it. It was a text message from a number I didn't recognize. The message was actually a link.

Weston leaned closer. "I don't know if it's a good idea to click on that."

As if someone had heard him, words appeared.

You'll want to see this.

I swallowed hard, not liking the implications of where this was going.

My fingers hovered over the link a moment.

When I finally clicked on it, it took me to a video—a livestream, actually.

I narrowed my eyes as I tried to process what I was seeing.

The video appeared to be taken of a dark parking lot. Two people stood near a truck, huddled close together.

I sucked in a breath.

Wait . . . that was me and Weston.

In real time.

I glanced around, looking for a sign of anyone who might be watching us right now.

Thirty minutes later, Weston and I hadn't been able to identify who had been recording the video. We'd slipped inside his truck, where our every movement couldn't be seen. But we hadn't left. Instead, we'd studied everything around us.

We knew the basic direction the video was being taken from—near a six-story apartment building with probably forty windows facing us.

The person recording this could be in any one of those.

I studied each one, but I didn't see any movement.

We'd called the police, and Detective Garrison arrived ten minutes after the video link had been sent. His guys went to search the building.

As soon as they did, the live video ended.

Garrison stood beside Weston on the driver's side of the truck. He'd taken my phone and was watching the feed until it finished.

"I'd like to see the whole video," Garrison muttered.

I waited a couple of minutes for the video to load before I pressed Play. Then I leaned closer and held my breath as I watched along with Weston and Garrison. The video started with Weston and I walking toward his truck.

I watched as he touched my arm. Watched as we hugged and leaned into one another.

Anyone subscribed to this channel could see the same things.

My private life was on display for anyone who might have the opportunity to watch.

And that wasn't okay.

As it ended again, Garrison stepped back and let

out a sigh. "I'll check with my IT guys and see if we can trace who this channel belongs to."

I nodded, but I knew there was little chance this person would be caught. Whoever was behind this was smart. No doubt he or she had figured out a way to do this without being located.

"Any idea why someone might want to record you two?" Garrison stared at me a moment before glancing at Weston.

Finally, Weston answered. "It could just be because of who we are. There are people who are obsessed with the idea of the two of us getting back together. Or the recording could be connected with the case Camryn has been investigating."

"The case?" Garrison's eyebrows flew up. "I take it that means you're officially looking into it, despite my discouragement."

I didn't say anything. He already knew the answer.

Garrison rubbed his chin before locking gazes with me. "This has happened more than once: you get involved, and then you put yourself in harm's way. I don't like that."

"I'm not trying to put myself in harm's way," I said, an edge of defensiveness in my voice. "I'm just trying to find answers."

"Maybe you should think twice about doing that."

I raised my chin, not liking it when people told me what to do. I wasn't outwardly defiant, but some intrinsic part of me rebelled when people with no authority over me tried to tell me what I should and shouldn't do.

"Did you guys find anyone up in that apartment building?" Weston swiftly changed the subject.

Garrison's jaw flexed before he shook his head. "No. Not yet. But one of my guys just called and said there was a box of chicken on the roof. Pickard's Poultry."

At his words, my breath caught.

That box hadn't been left there on accident.

That had been left there because someone clearly wanted to send a message: back off or you'll end up like Annie.

Were the stakes really this cutthroat?

I already knew that answer.

It was a resounding yes.

CHAPTER
TWENTY-FIVE

THE NEXT MORNING, Weston had promised to come over. It was Saturday so neither of us had to work. In two weeks, the semester would officially be over, which would significantly free up my schedule.

Last night, my father hadn't come back to Weston's apartment. He'd had the decency to call Weston and let him know he would be spending the night elsewhere and that he'd come get his few meager belongings sometime this weekend.

I didn't ask any questions. I had told him he needed to leave Weston's, but part of me hadn't expected him to do that without a fight.

Now I didn't know where he was or where he was staying. But maybe that was a good thing. Maybe I needed to let go. I only hoped he wasn't staying at Julie's. Talk about muddying the waters . . .

I'd already talked to Jinky, and there were still no changes with Annie. I couldn't be certain, but I thought I'd read that the longer a person was in a coma, the less likely they'd have a positive outcome.

I prayed that wasn't the case, however.

Dave had called me back. He hadn't been able to trace any information about those messages, unfortunately. Whoever had posted them had covered their tracks.

I had checked my phone continually last night, halfway expecting to see more live videos. Maybe even one of me sleeping.

I shuddered at that thought.

But no more videos had come.

Still, I was shaken by last night's livestream of Weston and me. This morning, I'd searched various sites, trying to see if there was anything about that live video feed taken of Weston and me, to see if any media sources had caught wind of the video and posted some type of attention-grabbing headline about the two of us getting back together.

Weston and I weren't back together, and if we were, I'd want to stay far away from the media. Relationships didn't usually bloom in the spotlight. They seemed to wither instead.

I didn't see anything.

At nine, Weston showed up at my place with

bagels and coffee. I thanked him, resisting the urge to reach up and give him a kiss on the cheek.

It would feel natural to do so.

Again, I reminded myself I needed to be cautious right now. Yes, if he broke up with me, I would recover. I would rise again.

That's just what women did.

But that didn't mean I wanted to invite that into my life either.

"This looks great," I said instead.

I led him to the small kitchen table, where we sat down.

Even looking at him, I could tell something was on his mind.

But before I even took a sip of my coffee, he cleared his throat. "So, now that it's just you and me, I was hoping we could talk about us. I need to give the record label an answer soon."

I swallowed hard. "I know you've been wanting to chat, and we've had so much going on." A sudden case of nerves fluttered through me, and my hands flew through the air, demonstrating a long list.

As they did, my fingers caught the edge of the coffee cup. It teetered before spilling and sending light brown liquid all over the table.

Weston and I both jumped from our seats at the

same time. As we grabbed for some paper towels, our fingers touched.

We both paused.

I looked up at him, my heart pounding in my ears.

I liked Weston. I'd always liked Weston.

I mean, I put any feelings aside when I was married, of course. It wasn't that I was pining over him while being married to Phil.

But something undeniably powerful existed between us.

I grabbed the paper towels. "I should get that . . ."

I nodded toward the liquid that dripped onto the floor.

"Camryn . . ." Weston started.

I froze, wondering what he was going to say. Wondering what he would do.

Before he could finish that statement and before I could wipe up my spilled coffee, a frantic knock sounded at the door.

I resisted a sigh.

What now?

Skittles rushed into my apartment, her laptop computer in hand. "Did you see it?"

Dread formed in my stomach.

I prayed it wasn't another needless death by poisoning. And, on a lesser note, I also prayed it wasn't that video of me and Weston.

"What's going on?" I asked.

She started toward my dinette but then saw Weston wiping up the spill and changed course. Instead, she went to my coffee table and set her computer there. She sat on the couch, leaned forward, and clicked some keys.

I saw that Weston had the coffee taken care of, so I lowered myself beside Skittles instead.

I watched as a video came up. The background was bright—it wasn't dark like the video taken of me and Weston. At least, that was a relief.

But my eyes widened when I saw Desi Does.

"It's live," she announced. "He's posting a challenge at this very moment. Every time he gets another donation, he adds another layer of clothes. He's already wearing fifteen. He's coming back into this full force."

I watched as Desi added another shirt and promised to keep doing this for the next hour.

A strange way to make money, but whatever worked for him . . .

"Did he say why he took a break? Give any indications about what was going on in his life?" I asked.

Weston sat on the other side of Skittles, also watching the computer screen.

"He said it's been a tough few days, and he wanted to take some time off out of respect for Annie. But his words aren't very convincing."

Skittles' eyes were glued to the screen. "As soon as I saw this pop up, I knew you'd want to see it."

"I do. I wonder if the police are watching this also."

"I don't know," Skittles said. "But I've seen other videos that he's done, and he's not acting normal in this one. He keeps looking around and fidgeting. His background isn't his normal one either."

"So, he's in hiding," Weston said.

"That sounds like a good guess." Skittles nodded. "And I think he's stressed. He doesn't sound as self-assured as usual."

I studied the screen and had to agree. Desi wasn't acting the same as he did in his other videos. He didn't look as comfortable in front of the camera.

Anyone in his shoes would be shaken. Was that why he was acting strange? Or was there more to it?

As soon as the video ended, I waited for a couple of minutes for it to finish compressing and then I asked her to play it again from the start.

This time, I listened with purpose.

And I wasn't listening to his words.

Instead, I listened to everything in the background. I tried to tap into my hearing abilities to pick up on some context clues that might show us where he was.

Because in my mind, Desi was someone who might have some answers for us.

Thankfully, Skittles and Weston seemed to get the clue and didn't say much as I listened.

I closed my eyes, trying to tune everything else out.

I could hear a slight tick in the background. Probably a wall clock if I had to guess. Somewhere in the distance, a dog barked. But it didn't sound like it was coming from anywhere close to where Desi was filming. On occasion, Desi rubbed his hands against his hips, a nervous gesture.

But I was going to need more than that if I was going to have any type of concrete clue as to where he might be.

I knew it was a long shot, but I had to try.

Finally, I heard a pounding sound.

I sucked in a breath as I listened. I wanted to be certain before I said anything.

There it was again.

"Camryn?" Weston asked, his voice low.

"Do you hear that?" I asked quietly.

"Hear what?" Skittles spoke up. "The dog barking?"

"There's that. But I also hear pile driving."

"Pile driving?" Weston repeated. "Wait . . . now that you mention it, I think I can hear it too."

"They're putting in a new bridge over on the west side of town. I heard they've been pile driving during all the daylight hours trying to get it done," Skittles said.

I nodded, knowing she was right. "Desi's probably in that area."

I popped my eyes open and studied the video again. I noted the way the sunlight hit the left side of Desi's face.

Since it was only 9:00 a.m., that meant the sun was coming up in the east.

If I had to guess, Desi was staying in either a hotel or an apartment building with windows facing the east near the area where the bridge was being built.

It was something.

I didn't know about Weston or Skittles, but I planned on finding out if my theory was correct.

CHAPTER
TWENTY-SIX

WESTON OFFERED TO DRIVE, and Skittles and I agreed.

As we headed toward the part of town where the bridge was being constructed, I continued to study the video, listening for more clues. I also listened to the sounds around us to get an indication of how close we might be.

The art of listening wasn't an exact science. In fact, I was mostly going off instinct.

I hoped it didn't let me down.

"What about that building right there?" Skittles pointed to a three-story hotel farther up the road. The building was a boxy, brick structure that had been painted beige. All the trim and signage were brown, and a small amount of landscaping made the estab-lishment look a little more welcoming.

Finally, I nodded. "It's worth checking out. Can we pull into the parking lot?"

Weston obliged. We sat in a space facing the building, windows cracked.

I observed everything around the area—a small convenience store, the industrial area of the river, the street marred with potholes.

The pile driver was a good distance away, but the sounds easily echoed across the water. Similar to the video.

The way the sun hit the building also fit.

Skittles might be right. This could be the location we were looking for.

"Even if this is where Desi is, how are you going to find him?" Weston asked. "The hotel must have at least a hundred rooms."

I nibbled on my lip a moment before saying, "There has to be a way."

"The barking dog . . ." Skittles suggested, popping her head between our seats. "We heard it in the video. If we can hear the yapping from inside the hotel, maybe that will give us a clue."

"And so, then you're going to march up to every door, knock on it and ask if Desi Does is staying there?" Weston raised his eyebrows as he posed the question. "Even if you find him, what are you going to do?"

"*When* we find him, I just want to ask him some questions," I said. "I'm hoping he can give us some insight."

"Whatever you guys want, I'm here for you." He raised his cup of coffee, poised to take a sip. "I just want you to be careful."

I looked back up at the building, realizing exactly what I was about to do.

I was about to take my snooping to a whole new level, a level that Garrison probably would not approve of.

Then I thought about that video that had been posted last night of me and Weston. I wondered if the person who'd taken it was following us now.

At that thought, I glanced around.

I didn't see anyone suspicious.

But if that theory was right, then I could be putting Desi's life on the line.

That meant I needed to plan each of my steps carefully.

"Act like we belong here, and no one will ask any questions," I said as the three of us stepped into the shabby hotel lobby—one that looked as if it hadn't been updated since the eighties with its off-white wallpaper, dark wood trim, and plaid couches.

And the smell—mothballs. Not one of my favorite scents.

"Why do you sound like an expert at this?" Weston asked beside me.

I shrugged. Suddenly, I felt like I knew what I was doing—even though I had no idea.

He pulled down his baseball cap.

Smart move. The last thing we needed was for someone to recognize him.

We threw a quick wave to the middle-aged woman working behind the desk. As we headed toward the elevator, she barely gave us a glance.

Good. Maybe my plan would actually work. Our first obstacles had been overcome—no one had recognized Weston.

But I had no idea where I was going.

The building contained three floors. I figured I'd start at the top and work my way down.

"If we're going to find him, I need to listen," I told Weston and Skittles as we stepped off the elevator.

"We'll stay quiet," Weston told me.

We silently walked down the hall, but I stopped halfway down.

I heard it.

The barking dog.

The canine was definitely on this floor.

But that didn't mean I wouldn't be able to hear the sound from other floors also.

I needed to keep that in mind.

I briefly considered pulling the fire alarm. That would get everyone out of their rooms, but that would only be a last resort. The action seemed too desperate, too juvenile. Besides, it wasn't like finding Desi was a life-threatening situation. Not exactly, at least.

Instead, I stepped closer to the door on my right and put my ear to the wood.

On the other side I heard a man and a woman talking.

I ruled that room out.

I moved on to the next door where I clearly heard children inside.

I ruled that room out too.

The next room was silent—maybe empty. And the dog's barking was becoming fainter. I made a mental note of that fact.

Then I moved on to the next door. This one sounded like the TV was on.

Until I realized it wasn't a TV.

It was someone . . . making a video.

I was nearly certain it was Desi's voice.

I turned back to Weston and Skittles and gave

them a nod.

Then I raised my hand and knocked at the door before yelling, "Housekeeping!"

As the word left my lips, I rolled my eyes.

I felt ridiculous using that excuse, like I'd watched too many movies or something.

Did anyone even fall for that trick anymore?

I was about to find out.

"I DON'T NEED ANY HOUSEKEEPING," Desi's deep voice called from the other side.

"Housekeeping!" I called again, pretending I hadn't heard.

Skittles grinned and gave me a thumbs-up, her stamp of approval.

On the other side of the door, Desi continued talking as if he were making another video. He didn't want to be interrupted, did he? But I was sure he didn't want my voice in his live feed either.

I knocked again and called, "Housekeeping!"

He groaned and excused himself.

Good. It sounded like he was slowly treading to the door.

Desi was probably still doing a livestream—which meant I needed to be careful.

The last thing I wanted was for anyone to pick up on our conversation.

Desi threw the door open, his eyes slitted with annoyance. He looked twenty pounds heavier wearing all those layers of clothes—including three baseball hats.

A smell hit me—the musty scent of second-hand store clothing.

He'd gotten everything at a thrift store and hadn't taken the time to wash any of it, if I had to guess.

"Look, you're going to have to come back—" Desi stopped mid-sentence when he saw the three of us.

Clearly, we were not dressed in housekeeping uniforms, nor did we have a trolley with any cleaning supplies next to us.

"Who are you?" His voice suddenly deepened, and he took a step back as if nervous.

I feared at any moment he might slam the door closed and our chance might be gone. I couldn't let that happen.

"We need to talk to you." I locked my gaze with his. "It's urgent."

"I don't want to talk to you." He started to shut the door, but I stuck my foot out to stop him.

"Please. It's important. And it needs to be private. I know you're streaming right now."

His eyes widened. "I muted it. Nobody can hear this."

"You need to stop the livestream." Weston stepped closer, his shoulders bristled and his voice firm.

Desi glanced up, and his eyes widened with recognition. "Aren't you . . . ?"

"Weston Turner. Yes, I am. You've got to know we'd only come here if it was urgent."

Desi stared at us one more moment before nodding. "At least, tell me what this is about first."

"It's about Annie King," I told him. "We're trying to figure out who tried to kill her."

Skittles double-checked Desi's computer to make sure he wasn't still recording. That was the last thing we needed right now.

Then Skittles and I perched on the edge of a double bed and faced Desi as he sat across from us on the other bed. Weston stood a few feet back, near the door as if preventing an escape attempt.

Desi, with his dark hair and olive complexion, looked surprisingly pale. Though he had a stocky build, something about him seemed gaunt right now.

"I don't know what you want me to tell you." His

words came out fast. "I was really sad to hear about Annie."

"When was the last time you saw her?" I asked.

His eyebrows shot up as if he instantly put together the fact I thought he could be guilty.

"It's been at least a week." His words came out even faster. "Way before all this happened. Why?"

"Where did you see her?" I continued to press.

"Whoa, whoa, whoa!" He raised his hands in the air as if he was being attacked. "What's with all these questions? And how did you even find me here?"

"There were all kinds of clues in your videos," Skittles told him. "And Camryn is the best."

"I was careful not to show anything except a blank background." He still sounded unconvinced.

"To anyone who is carefully watching and listening, you can hear the pile driving in the background," I told him. "Hear the dog. See how the sunlight hits your face."

Desi grunted and scratched his head as if he hadn't considered that.

"Now, about Annie," I continued, trying to keep the impatience from my voice. "When was the last time you saw her?"

"Like I said, it was a week ago. I went to her apartment so we could talk."

"Did Celeste know about that?" Skittles asked. "She seems like the jealous type."

"Me and Celeste are through."

"Why did you guys break up?" Weston stepped closer and stood with hands on his hips giving Desi the stare down.

He was much better at being intimidating than I'd ever known.

And I kind of liked it.

"It just wasn't working out." His eyes shifted as if he didn't like this topic of conversation. "We were too similar. We tried to make it work for the sake of our careers, but it wasn't worth it."

At least, he had enough sense to realize that.

I wasn't sure he was telling the complete truth, but I had other questions. "Back to Annie. You met her at her apartment a week ago to talk about something. What was it?"

He stared in the distance before letting out a long, burdened breath. "I stopped by to see if we could get back together. Okay? Are you happy now?"

"What did Annie say?" I ignored the irritation in his voice.

"She said no and told me to get out. That was it."

"So, why are you hiding right now?" I continued. "Because that's clearly what you're doing."

Desi glanced around as if nervous someone else

might be listening. "I've been getting some threats. Then when I heard what happened to Annie, I realized that maybe the threats weren't all empty."

"What kind of threats?" Weston narrowed his eyes with thought.

"The same kind that Annie had been getting." Desi paused as guilt flooded his gaze. "Lavern told me about them. That's the only reason I knew what was going on."

Lavern? What?

The two of them were talking?

Why hadn't I heard about this before?

Emotions churned inside me, but I tried not to be too reactive.

"Why would Lavern tell you about that?" Skittles scoffed. "What kind of a friend is she to do something like that?"

Desi let out another heavy sigh. "Lavern came over to confront me, to see if I was the one who'd been sending the threats to Annie. And I wasn't."

"Why would she think that you were?" I countered, trying to form a better picture of what was happening.

"You'll have to ask her that." Desi crossed his arms. "Sometimes maybe I get a little too competitive. But I'd *never* want to hurt Annie. I'm not like that."

"Not even over the endorsement deal?" I asked.

He blanched. "What endorsement deal?"

I stared at him a moment. He didn't know about it. Not if my instincts were right.

In fact, Desi was frightened. I could hear it in his voice. The threats and the attempt on Annie's life had shaken him to the core.

But was he also hiding something?

That's what I needed to figure out.

CHAPTER
TWENTY-EIGHT

WESTON, Skittles, and I sat in his truck after we'd left Desi's hotel room. I didn't know about Weston and Skittles, but my thoughts were racing after our conversation with Desi.

"What are you thinking?" Weston shifted toward me in the driver's seat.

I let out a breath. "My thoughts are muddled, unfortunately."

"Then let's talk through them," Weston said. "Who are your suspects?"

I loved the way he thought sometimes. He was able to sense my emotions and help channel them, help me to focus.

He'd been like this when I used to get stage fright. He was one of the only people who'd been able to calm me down. I'd always appreciated that about him.

I scanned the landscape around us, halfway afraid someone was still watching. When I saw no one, I started.

"First, there's Lavern," I said. "I don't want to believe she's guilty. But the police believe she is. She did handle Annie's food, so she had means and opportunity. As far as motive, she got upset with Annie and posted that comment online. *Some days are amazing and other days I'd like to strangle my boss.*"

"But you can't take that literally," Skittles reminded me, popping her head forward from the backseat.

"No, you can't. And Lavern seems truly shaken."

"Could that simply be regret?" Weston stretched his arm across the back of the seat.

"I can't rule that out." I frowned after saying the words. I didn't want Lavern to be guilty. But I needed to be open-minded also. "Then there's Celeste. She's over-the-top competitive, and Annie's demise could mean her own rise to fame. Plus, maybe she's jealous because Annie and Desi dated."

"That seems extreme," Weston said.

"It is." I nodded slowly. "But people have committed crimes for crazier reasons than jealousy."

"Keep going," Weston crossed his arms and listened.

"Then there's Penelope. Out of the blue, Annie fired her. She also seemed to be truly grieving. But what if she's hiding something?"

"From what you've told me, she doesn't seem like the vengeful type," Weston said.

"That's how she struck me also." I let out one more long breath. "And that leaves me with Desi. Annie didn't want to get back together with him. Was he so angry about her rejection that he wanted to kill her?"

"Good question," Skittles said. "And we still have to think about who had the opportunity to put rat poison in the batter for the fried chicken. As my mom always said, 'The one who holds the spice holds the flavor.'"

I wasn't really sure about the wisdom behind her advice, but she did have a point.

"You're right," I said. "That's the key to it all. Who would have been able to add that rat poison? It also makes me wonder if it was someone who knew about the endorsement deal. Pickard's Poultry and fried chicken? It can't be a coincidence."

"I agree," Weston said. "Someone was sending a message."

"Didn't you say something about someone threatening Annie, that if she didn't send fifty thousand dollars her secrets would be exposed?" Skittles said. "Who sent that note? What secrets were they referring to? And whatever happened?"

I leaned back into my seat, grateful that Weston had started his truck and cool air blew through the vents. The sun came in on my side of the vehicle, heating my skin. "That's one clue we haven't fully explored, isn't it? I don't even know where to start. Would Lavern, Desi, Celeste, or Penelope send that? Who would know secrets about Annie?"

"They could all potentially know some secrets about her," Skittles said.

"What could Annie possibly be hiding?" I continued. "The same secrets Krissy Stovall had? Only Krissy was killed. What's the connection?"

We sat in silence a moment.

I didn't know the answers to those questions.

I wasn't even sure where to find them.

I could ask the same old people the same old questions. But I had a feeling I wouldn't get any different answers.

I needed a new lead.

As I glanced up at a car pulling into the parking lot, I realized I'd just gotten one.

"Is that . . . ?" Skittles' voice trailed.

"Celeste," I finished. My gaze latched onto the woman as she walked across the lot wearing oversized joggers, a midriff-baring pink T-shirt, and oversized sunglasses.

But it was clearly Celeste.

"What's *she* doing here?" Skittles continued to stare at the woman in disbelief.

"If I had to guess, she's here to see Desi." Weston rubbed his jaw as he shook his head. "The two of them definitely have something up their sleeves."

Before anyone could stop me, I opened the truck door and scurried outside.

Weston and Skittles followed close behind me.

Just as Celeste reached the sidewalk, I stepped into her path, blocking it, and crossed my arms. "Fancy seeing you here."

Her skin paled when she recognized me. "What are you doing here?"

"I just had a nice, long conversation with Desi. You?"

"It's not what you think." Her voice trembled, and she took a step back.

"I'm really tired of people telling me that." I wasn't even exaggerating. Why couldn't people just tell the truth the first time?

"But it's true! Desi and I . . . our breakup . . . it was just a stunt to get more views!"

"How would that get more views?" I was truly perplexed.

Celeste glanced around as if nervous she was being watched. "People love drama. Drama gets attention. Being happy? There's no drama in that. So, we staged this breakup."

"But Desi said he tried to get back together with Annie." Skittles stepped closer, her tone no-nonsense.

Celeste's lips parted as if she hadn't expected Skittles' statement. "That was just a stunt. His subscribers paid him ten thousand dollars to do it."

"What?" Disbelief captured my voice. People would really do that? "Why?"

"His subscribers tell him everything—what to wear, eat, how to act. It's part of his schtick."

"If that's true, why didn't that relationship drama ever air on his channel?" Weston asked.

"The day he had it scheduled was the day Annie almost died. He couldn't post it then. It would have been highly insensitive."

"But he recorded the whole thing?" I clarified.

Celeste frowned. "I know this sounds horrible, but yes. He recorded the whole thing. He wore a little camera hidden on his watch."

"You both should be ashamed of yourselves." I

couldn't help it. My mothering side was coming out. What Celeste and Desi had done was downright deplorable.

Besides, something about the whole setup smelled fishy to me.

I stepped closer. "Where were you when Krissy died?"

Celeste's skin grew even paler. "Alone. In my apartment. I wasn't even online."

No alibi. That could definitely work against her.

"Did you know about the endorsement deal?" I continued.

"Endorsement deal?"

But I saw the truth flicker in her gaze. She knew about it.

"The one with Pickard's Poultry," I prodded.

"I don't know what you're talking about."

"I think you do." I locked gazes with her.

Celeste raised her chin. "Talk to Lavern."

"I've already been talking to Lavern." I wasn't sure where she was going with this.

"Lavern called me right after Annie went into the hospital, and she asked if she could work for me. If I were you, she's the person I'd be looking at. Now, I need to run."

Then Celeste darted into the hotel before we could ask her anything else.

TWENTY-NINE

WESTON and I dropped Skittles off. She had to get ready for a K-Pop concert this evening that she'd bought tickets to six months ago.

Weston told me his schedule was open, so I asked him to swing by Lavern's place.

I still had more questions for her. I didn't have anything else slated for today, and I felt close to finding answers.

Julie answered the door, wearing fitted jeans and a pale blue top. Her makeup and hair were already done, and she wore strappy sandals.

She was just my father's type.

I didn't know whether to pity her or resent her for going out to eat with my father.

Probably neither reaction was right. I just needed to take the whole situation in stride.

"You're here for Lavern?" Julie asked as she stood in the doorway. "Unfortunately, she's not in a good headspace right now. Everything is really getting to her, to say the least, and she's lying down. I keep trying to talk her into going home with me, but she insists on staying here in Savannah."

"Julie, do you know if Lavern was aware of the endorsement deal Annie was offered?" I studied the woman's face, searching for the truth.

"Endorsement deal?" She cocked an eyebrow. "Why would Annie get an endorsement deal?"

"Some people with strong social media followings get them," Weston explained.

Julie let out a disbelieving chuckle. "Well, I had no idea. All I know is what Lavern tells me."

"Are you sure I can't talk to Lavern?" I asked.

"She really does need her sleep. It's important to her mental health, you know? And she's been through so much."

I nodded. "I understand. Could you ask her to call as soon as she wakes up?"

Julie smiled, even though the action looked tight and forced. "Of course."

I started to step away when she called to me again.

I turned toward her and saw what almost looked like an apology in her gaze. Her eyes had softened as had her shoulders. "I know it's prob-ably weird that I went out to dinner with your father."

So many thoughts went through my head. I wanted to warn her to stay away from my dad. To tell her my father's history. To give her a good shake.

I did none of those things.

Instead, I nodded and waited.

"I think he seems like a really good guy," Julie said. "I know he messed up in the past. But we all can change, right?"

After a moment of reluctance, I finally said, "He hasn't proven that yet."

"Well, what better time than now? I mean, I hate people who take advantage of others, just as much as anyone. But second chances are beautiful." Her eyes lifted as if that thought made her happy.

I was all in favor of people being happy. What I didn't want to see was that happiness turn into pain. However, Julie was an adult. I couldn't tell her what to do. Nor could I control my dad. The only thing that made me feel better was knowing that my dad had agreed not to date her anymore.

But was he telling the truth?

"I hope you're right," I finally said. "But I'd be careful if I were you."

"I will be."

I hoped she didn't pursue anything else with my dad.

Because she had no idea who she was up against.

But I'd tried to warn her. I'd asked Dad to stay away. I'd done all I could do.

Now, I had to step back and hope for the best.

As Weston and I left Lavern's, I glanced at my watch and saw it was past lunchtime. I volunteered to treat him to a meal. It was the least that I could do considering all the time and effort he'd put into helping me.

We stopped at a restaurant called Kiss My Grits. Their specialty? Grits, of course. Their shrimp and grits was my favorite.

The place was located on the water, surrounded by marsh grass. The inside was clean and simple with shiplap walls and a rustic farmhouse style of decorating.

As we were seated at a corner table by the window, the scent of Old Bay and shrimp filled the air, something about it bringing me surprising comfort.

Our drinks came quickly, and we ordered our food. As the waitress scurried off to another table, Weston and I settled in to talk.

Weston held his straw and made circles in his sweet iced tea as he looked at me. "What a day, huh?"

"What a week. None of this was on my agenda. Jinky simply asked me to look into the threats against Annie, and now look where we are." I shrugged, honestly in disbelief.

"I think fate is trying to tell you that maybe you picked the wrong career. Maybe a career in investigating was supposed to be in your future."

I shrugged again. "I don't know about that. But details are kind of my thing. And I enjoy helping people."

A slow grin stretched across his face. "I can tell. I think it's great you've finally realized that. And to be honest, it's been kind of fun being your sidekick. It's been a nice change of pace."

"Change of pace?"

He shrugged and glanced to the side as he gathered his thoughts. "I'm used to people wanting to cater to me. It's the nature of life in the spotlight. But then I came here to Grand Isle, which has offered a nice balance in my life. But there are still people who treat me like royalty. Not you."

I squirmed. "Should I apologize?"

He chuckled. "No, absolutely not. That didn't

come out as I intended. I just mean that you make me feel normal. And I want to feel normal."

I wasn't sure exactly where he was going with this.

"Something about you has always grounded me. You've never cared about my fame or my money. In fact, I think you'd be more attracted to me if I didn't have those things." Weston cast an almost sad smile. "I've always known that you liked me for me, and I appreciate that."

I feel my cheeks warm. "I would have liked you no matter what. In fact, when we were dating, you were poor. We both were."

We exchanged a smile.

Weston paused and stared at me another moment. "Isn't it funny how time brought us back to the very same place where we started?"

My heart beat harder. I thought I knew where he was going with this conversation. But when I set aside my emotions, I heard the truth in his words.

"You're right. I never thought the two of us would end up back here." I pushed a lock of hair behind my ear. "Grand Isle has a lot of great memories, doesn't it?"

"It really does." The warmth in Weston's eyes made my heart flutter and my skin flush.

I'd always loved it when he looked at me like

that. It made me feel like the only woman in the whole world. Despite all our problems. Our past. My lack of trust. My fear over new relationships.

When he stared at me as he was in this moment, everything else disappeared.

Our food was served, and we prayed together before eating. My creamy grits mixed with the spicy shrimp, peppers, and sausage was like an orchestra on my tongue, each flavor a note and every new spice a rising crescendo.

I loved every bite.

Weston had gotten grits covered with a soft fried egg and crispy bacon. He took a bite and wiped his mouth before turning toward me. "I thought you should know that I made a decision about that tour."

Everything went still around me.

My heart pounded in my ears as I waited. Antici-pated. Dreaded.

Had he just brought up fate bringing us back together at Grand Isle as a transition to life leading us in separate directions?

Anxiety thrummed inside me.

"As I told you before, I need to call the label back and let them know what I want to do," Weston continued. "Today is the day."

I swallowed, my food seeming to lodge in my

throat. I took a sip of my tea as I waited for him to continue.

He leaned closer and lowered his voice. "Camryn, I just want to tell you how much you've always meant to me . . ."

I knew where this was going.

Weston was about to tell me he was leaving.

All that talk about coming back here so he could spend more time with his kids? Had it just been a flash in the pan? A whim?

Because his kids were still here. And they still needed him.

Maybe I was beginning to need him also—I just hadn't realized it until now.

Panic began to flutter up inside me.

"The truth is . . ." he started.

Before Weston could finish his statement, my phone rang.

Interruptions seemed to be happening at the worst of times lately, weren't they?

I would have ignored the call, but when I glanced at the screen, I saw Jinky's name.

"Do you mind?" I felt rude even asking the question. If it wasn't for everything going on with Annie, I wouldn't. But I feared bad news considering Annie's precarious situation.

"Go ahead." But his disappointment was clear in the frown that tugged at his lips.

I'd have to deal with that in a moment.

Right now, I put the phone to my ear. Before I could even say hello, Jinky spoke.

"You'll never believe this," she started. "But Annie is awake. And she's talking."

CHAPTER
THIRTY

WESTON and I paused in the hospital waiting room until I spotted Jinky step inside. The brightest smile I'd seen on her face in a long time greeted me.

I hurried toward her and pulled her into a hug. "This is great news."

She pulled away and practically beamed at me as she said, "Isn't it?"

"So, she just woke up?" Weston stepped closer.

Jinky nodded enthusiastically. "That's right. It's like a miracle. I was afraid we were going to have to make some end-of-life decisions. But Annie opened her eyes as Nancy and I were standing in the room with her. A few minutes later, the nurses took the breathing tube out and Annie started talking, almost like she'd just been taking a nap or something. It was crazy—but a good kind of crazy."

"I know you're thrilled. This is what we've been praying for."

"Yes, it is. Do you want to see her?"

My eyebrows shot up. Of course, I wanted to see her. But I had enough manners to know I shouldn't lead with that.

"I'm sure she needs some time to recover," I said instead.

"She wants to know who did this to her. She actually said she wanted to talk to you."

My eyebrows climbed higher. "Really?"

Jinky nodded. "Really."

"Okay then. If she thinks she's ready, then I'm all ears." That could be my new catch phrase. All ears.

I mentally shook my head at the thought.

"I'll wait here for you." Weston nodded at a nearby chair.

We hadn't finished our conversation in his truck. Instead, I'd rambled on and on with questions about Annie and how she was doing and what had happened.

Was it a purposeful diversion? Maybe on a subconscious level it was. Maybe I didn't want to hear that Weston was leaving again just as we'd reconnected.

But the important thing right now was that Annie had awoken.

I followed Jinky down the hall and into a hospital room. Then I prayed I'd find the right questions to ask her.

After several minutes of preliminary conversation, Annie's gaze met mine and held. "You need to figure out who did this to me."

I stepped closer, hearing the unmistakable challenge in her voice. "That's exactly what I want to do. I'm hoping you might have some insights."

She licked her dry, cracked lips before shaking her head. "But I don't. I mean, there are other influencers who are competitive with me. I'm sure you've talked to Celeste. There are haters out there, trolls if you will, who are only happy if they're being jerks to other people. Then there are the people I've made mad just because of business decisions that I've made."

I swallowed hard as I attempted to broach the subject. "You mean like when you fired Penelope?"

Annie shrugged. "Maybe. But I've always liked Penelope. We didn't really end our working relationship on a bad note. She just wasn't very good at what she did."

"How did she handle that news?"

Annie shrugged again. "Not well, as you can imagine. It was hard on me having to let her go. But I knew that was what I needed to do."

"You hired Lavern. I guess you trusted her."

"Of course. She's my friend."

"She seems to think you told the police she could have been the one sending you those threats." I waited to see how she responded.

"I didn't want to throw her under the bus. But they asked about anyone at all who'd made any kind of threat. After I told them about her post, I insisted it couldn't be her."

"How about Desi?" I moved right into my next question.

Annie let out a long sigh, suddenly seeming more uncertain than before. "We have a complicated history. I'm not sure if he ever really liked me at all or if our relationship was a publicity stunt. I feel certain his breakup was done for ratings as well as when he tried to reconcile with me."

Relief washed through me. At least, she already knew that, and I didn't have to break that news. "Did you know you were being recorded when he asked to get back together with you?"

She shrugged, but there was no surprise on her features. "I figured as much. Really, at that point, I just wanted to get Desi out of my house. I knew he and Celeste were talking, and I knew he was desperate. More than anything, he wanted to make it big, and he wasn't going to let anyone stand in his way."

"What about that endorsement deal?" I had a long list of questions for her, and I hated to hit her with them rapid-fire. But time wasn't on our side.

If someone had done this to her, who was to say they wouldn't return to finish what they started?

She shrugged as if it weren't a big deal. "I didn't tell anybody about it because I wanted to make sure it was what I wanted to do first. Pickard's Poultry really isn't my favorite restaurant, and I needed to come to terms with whether or not I could endorse them. It was as simple as that."

She made it sound so casual, almost like it wasn't a reason for someone to poison her.

But I wasn't so sure about that.

I moved closer before asking my final question. "Annie . . . who was threatening to expose your secrets? And—I hate to ask this but—what were those secrets?"

Before Annie could answer, a nurse had come in to check her vitals. I tried to wait patiently throughout the process.

But I was anxious to hear her response.

Finally, the nurse left, and it was just me, Annie, and Jinky again.

Annie sobered as she turned back to me. "You know about those threats?"

I nodded. "I do. Penelope saw the note on your desk. She said she wasn't snooping, but that she accidentally came across it."

"It wasn't my proudest moment." Annie stared out the window a moment before turning back to me. "In fact, I just want to pretend like it never happened."

"What are you talking about?" I shifted my weight, curious to see where she was going with this.

"It happened about six months ago down in Florida." Annie's voice trembled. "I had gone down to party with some of my friends. It was right after Desi and I broke up, and I really wanted to blow off some steam."

I waited for her to continue, a bad feeling swirling in my gut.

"We went into a restaurant down there—one that foodies up and down the coast love." Annie's eyes misted. "I was *so* looking forward to trying the food there and maybe even featuring it in some way on my channel. Unfortunately, before I arrived, I'd already had a few drinks. I was pretty tipsy when I got to the restaurant."

Drinks had a way of doing that to people. "Go on."

Annie rubbed her throat as if she didn't want to continue. But a moment later, her gaze met mine again.

"I got pretty nasty with the waitress at the restaurant," Annie said. "It wasn't that she was terrible. It was just that I was unhappy, and I needed someone to take it out on. I said some unkind things to her before storming out of the restaurant."

"And . . . ?" Clearly, there was more to this story.

"Someone who'd been in the restaurant caught it all on video. They sent me that footage and said they were going to put it on YouTube if I didn't pay up. I've known other influencers who've gone down for lesser things before, and I knew that this could ruin everything. I wasn't willing to let that happen."

"So, you paid up?"

She nibbled on her bottom lip before nodding. "I did. It took almost all the money I'd saved. I had to start using my credit cards, which I soon maxed out. I needed to build my cash supply back up, which was why that endorsement deal was so tempting. I needed the cash."

"Annie . . ." Jinky whispered with a tilt of her head. "I would have helped you."

"I know." She shrugged, tears of shame filling her gaze. "I just wanted to figure it out myself. I wanted to dig myself out of the hole, you know?"

I hated that she had to do that . . . and I hated it more that someone was getting away with it.

"Did you ever have any clue who it was who sent you that extortion?" I asked. "Have you tried to track it?"

Annie's gaze met mine as she shook her head. "I have no idea who was behind it, and I've tried to keep it under wraps, so no one knows . . . except me and the person who made the demands."

MY MIND RACED as I headed back to the waiting area.

Weston rose as soon as he saw me step into the room. "Is Annie okay?"

I remembered the bright-eyed girl sitting up in her hospital bed. "She barely even seemed groggy. It's amazing."

He stepped closer. "I'm so glad to hear that. What now?"

"I'm sure you probably have other things to do . . ." Weston had been so, so patient about this. And even though he said he enjoyed being my sidekick, I knew he had limits. Everyone did.

"The kids are with me next weekend. But this weekend I'm free, and I'm all yours."

Warmth rushed through me. He sounded as if he honestly enjoyed spending time with me.

To be truthful—I enjoyed spending time with him also.

I wished I had nothing better to do than to relish that realization.

But I couldn't, not when so much was on the line.

My thoughts continued to wander, and I nibbled on my bottom lip as I tried to sort through them. I wanted my mind to settle, to focus. But it felt like a tornado ripped through my brain instead, turning everything upside down.

"What is it?" Weston narrowed his eyes as he studied me.

"There's something bugging me. Something I think we've been missing as we've been concentrating on each of the suspects."

"What is it?"

I glanced around, making sure no one else was nearby. "I don't know, but something is nagging me. I can't quite pinpoint what exactly it is yet. I feel like there's a realization on the verge of emerging."

"Take a few deep breaths. Maybe it will come to you."

In the middle of my second deep breath, my phone rang . . . again. When I saw it was my dad, I hesitated. I wanted to ignore it, but that didn't seem very mature.

Finally, I ripped the Band-Aid off and answered. "What's up, Dad?"

"Camryn . . . I know you're probably a little upset with me still, but I ran into a little snafu with my new living situation. I wondered if I might be able to go to your apartment for an hour or two to freshen up. I promise to stay out of your hair."

I closed my eyes, wishing he wasn't putting me in this position. "I'd say yes, but I'm not going to be home to give you a key."

I sent Weston a look as he seemed to pick up on our conversation. He frowned as if realizing my dad was being manipulative again.

"I can get in."

My shoulders stiffened. "How would you do that?"

"I have a key."

"What? How did you get a key?" I searched my memories from when that might have happened.

"I found a spare one in your drawer when I was at your place. I assumed at that point I would be staying with you, so I slipped it into my pocket and then forgot about it. Now that seems to be working out in my favor."

"I'm sure that's how you see it . . ." I muttered. I

should be surprised, but I wasn't. I tried to control the anger that simmered inside me. "Dad—"

"Look, I'm sorry. But I need somewhere to go. I'll only be there for an hour. Two at the most."

He was my father. He needed a hand. And I had an apartment close by.

What kind of daughter would I be if I said no?

"Fine." My jaw stiffened as I said the word. "But only because I'm not going to be home for a while. But you said you had your own place, right? What's the snafu about?"

"There are just a few more details I'm trying to work out. I promise." Dad's voice sounded convincing.

Even though I saw through him, I could still see why others fell for his act. He put on a good show. But I didn't have time to worry about this right now.

"Fine. Just don't touch anything, got it?"

"Understood."

As soon as I hit End, my phone beeped again. This time it was Lavern.

It had been a long time since I'd been this popular.

"My mom said you stopped by." Her voice sounded listless, as if she were struggling with depression.

I might have just the cure for her.

"Did you hear about Annie?" I paced toward the corner as another family filled the waiting room.

"What about her?" Lavern's voice caught as if she were worried.

"She's awake." I listened closely, hoping to hear any changes in Lavern's voice after the revelation.

"What?" Lavern almost sounded breathless with relief. "That's fantastic. Can I see her?"

She sounded honestly surprised and happy. I had no indication she was faking any of the emotions I heard in her voice.

"You'll have to run that through her mom and Jinky," I told her. "I'm not sure. But I thought you'd want to know."

"That's the best news I've heard all day. Annie will set this straight. She knows I'd never do anything to hurt her." Hope filled her tone.

I wanted Lavern to have her moment—if she was innocent. But I still had more questions.

"Lavern, I heard you were also friends with Krissy Stovall. Is that right?"

She didn't say anything for a moment. I could nearly hear her heart pounding, her breathing becoming more rapid.

"The two of us weren't close," she finally said.

At least, she hadn't lied again.

"After what happened to Annie, did you really

call Celeste to see if you might be able to work for her if things didn't work out for Annie?"

"I was just trying to stay on top of things." Lavern's voice cracked. "I have bills to pay, and I feel terrible about what happened to Annie. But if I don't pay my rent, then I'm going to get kicked out and have to move back in with my mom. That's the last thing that I want to do."

"I still might have a few questions for you," I said. "Can we meet?"

"I'd love to meet. How about in an hour? My mom is having a date over so I'm anxious to get out of this place. Believe me."

Her mom certainly liked to date around. She didn't waste any time, did she?

I glanced at Weston, who nodded at me. "Fine. Let's meet for coffee at The Family Bean. In an hour. Sound good?"

"Yes. Tell Annie I'm thinking about her. And that I would never do this to her."

"What are you thinking now?" Weston asked as we drove toward the coffeehouse.

I was so preoccupied with my thoughts that I barely heard him.

I was missing something. Maybe I was even missing *someone*. I was certain of it.

I felt like I was staring at one of those drawings where you're supposed to identify something that's out of place. Your eyes know something isn't right, but it takes a few minutes for your brain to process, to catch up.

That's what this mystery was like right now.

I glanced back at Weston. "Hear me out a minute. Maybe I just need to talk this through."

"Go right ahead."

I let out a long breath before diving in. "Whoever tried to kill Annie needed to be able to access rat poison, which is pretty readily available, right? But the key is they also had to be able to access the flour that was used for the fried chicken batter. On top of that, this person needs a motive."

"That's correct."

"I still have trouble trying to figure out how Celeste, Desi, or Penelope, would have access to that flour," I said. "Someone would have seen this person get so close."

"It does seem like somebody would have noticed if someone suspicious was hovering nearby," Weston agreed.

I leaned back in my seat, thoughts still racing. "Whoever is behind this wanted to put Annie out of commission as well as Krissy. Originally, we thought it was because someone else wanted to be in the limelight. But what if that wasn't the case at all? What if it was somebody who wanted to get Annie and Krissy out of the way for another reason?"

Weston threw a glance my way. "Okay. I can see where you're going with this. But who? And why?"

"I have no idea. Who else would have a reason to stop them? Lavern?"

"Lavern *does* have a lot to lose."

I shook my head as I stared out the window at the passing landscape and chewed on that thought. "Maybe. And I know I've thought about that theory myself. But I don't think Lavern did this."

"What do you think happened then?"

I raced through all the clues, visualizing each possible suspect before stopping on one face.

My heart pounded in my ears. My breath caught. My lungs tightened.

I was wrong.

Right?

I had to be.

But I didn't think I was.

I prided myself in being able to hear inconsistencies in people's voices.

Yet I'd missed a big one.

"Camryn?"

I glanced at Weston. "We're going to need to change course."

"What?"

I nodded slowly, still in a state of disbelief myself. "I think I know who did it."

I CALLED Garrison as Weston and I headed down the road. I knew I didn't want to be like the boy who cried wolf. But I felt nearly certain my theory was correct.

The detective promised to be on his way and asked me not to make any moves.

I bypassed the coffeehouse and instead went to Lavern's apartment, where I pounded on the door.

But no one answered.

Yes, I knew I said I'd wait. But I couldn't just stand here.

Especially since Lavern had told me her mom was going to have dinner tonight with someone.

My heart beat harder as I pounded my fist on the wooden door one more time. "Why isn't she answering? Julie is supposed to be here with a date."

Weston put his hand on my arm. "Maybe there's a good reason."

"I need to call Lavern. See if she knows anything." I pulled out my phone and quickly dialed her number. Lavern answered right away. "Hey, listen. Something came up, and I'm going to have to wait on that coffee. In the meantime, do you know where your mom is?"

"She said her date got rescheduled and they were going to go somewhere else to eat. Why?"

"Did she say where they were going?" I rushed.

"Not specifically. What's going on? Why do you sound so frantic?"

I leaned against the hallway wall, my thoughts racing. "It's important that I find her, Lavern. You have no idea where she is?"

"No. I'm sorry, but I don't."

There had to be a way to figure it out. "Do you know who her date was with?"

"If I understood her correctly it was . . . your dad."

The breath left my lungs.

Was Julie on a date with my dad because she truly liked him?

I had a hard time believing that.

Especially when I thought about some of the

things she'd said—including the statement, "I hate when people try to take advantage of others."

That defined my father.

What if Julie somehow wanted to get revenge on my dad after she'd caught onto his scheme?

A humming started between my ears.

"Camryn?"

I glanced up and saw Weston staring at me.

"I think Julie's with my dad," I rushed. "I don't think it's because she likes him. I think it's because she wants to teach him a lesson."

The words sounded surreal as they left my lips.

Maybe I was overreaching here . . . but I didn't think I was.

Weston's eyes widened. "If you're right, where would they be?"

"That's what I need to figure out." My mind raced through all the possibilities. "Let me try to call him."

I dialed his number, but the call went to voice mail.

My heart thrummed harder.

Just then, Garrison appeared at the end of the hallway. A questioning look captured his expression —from the knot between his eyes to the frown on his face—as he approached me.

"You really think that Lavern's mom is responsible?" He paused in front of me.

I nodded. "She's not answering, and Lavern doesn't know where she is."

He motioned to one of his guys. A few minutes later, he came back with the apartment manager who opened the door for us.

But the apartment appeared empty . . . except for a box of rat poison on the counter.

Rat poison?

Had that been left out on purpose? To send a message?

Or had Julie pulled it out to use it?

My heart beat harder.

"Where would she have gone?" Garrison turned toward me, his jaw flexing with displeasure.

"I don't know. I think she could be with my dad. And I think she's angry with him."

His gaze darkened. "I'll let patrol know. They'll keep their eyes open for them. I don't want to jump the gun here."

"I know." I swallowed hard, hardly able to breathe. "Thank you."

"And if you happen to find them . . . call us."

I nodded. "I will."

Weston and I walked back to his truck. But, instead of getting inside, he pulled me into his arms again. It was becoming a regular occurrence. I wasn't complaining.

"We'll find your dad," he murmured.

I didn't say anything. I hoped that was the case. I hoped he was okay.

But I didn't feel certain.

And I'd hate for our last conversation to be so negative.

"Like being bathed in sunshine, is the warmth you bring to me," he quietly sang in my ear. "Like a blanket over me on a cool and cloudy day, like honey on my tastebuds to drive my blues away . . ."

My heart beat harder. It was one of his top songs. One of the ones that had put him on the charts. And his voice sounded so perfectly smooth as he crooned the words.

Words meant for me.

A song he'd written for me when I'd struggled with my dad's choices twenty years ago.

As I pulled away from his embrace, I looked up at him.

That's when I realized I hadn't pulled away that far at all.

In fact, our faces were only inches apart.

Weston reached for me, and his hand skimmed

my cheek.

I leaned into his touch, desperate for comfort.

"It's going to be okay," he murmured.

"I hope so."

I thought he might kiss me. Part of me wanted him to.

But if we kissed, I wanted the moment to be right.

And this moment didn't feel right.

Not considering my dad might be in danger.

Weston looped some of my hair behind my ear. "Do you want to drive around town and look for them?"

Searching the area seemed like an exercise in futility.

I shrugged and glanced around, wishing an answer would magically drop in my lap. But I knew better.

"How about we go back to your apartment?" Weston suggested. "Maybe your dad left something there, some type of clue about where he was going."

"That's a great idea."

We hopped in his truck and drove to my place. Quickly, we hurried up the steps and to my door.

But as I grabbed my key, I froze.

Voices rang out from the other side.

One belonged to my dad.

The other belonged to . . . Julie.

CHAPTER
THIRTY-THREE

"WHAT DO YOU WANT TO DO?" Weston's gaze bore into mine.

I tried to subdue my panic. "First, we call Garrison and let him know. Then I need to go inside and try to buy some time. I don't know what Julie is planning, but I imagine it's not good. Best-case scenario is that I'm just being paranoid. Worst-case scenario is whatever she's planning has already been enacted."

Weston sucked in a breath as if hearing my words out loud startled him.

"Let me call Garrison." He pulled out his phone and dialed his number.

Garrison said he was on his way, and Weston ended the call before turning toward my door. He stared at it a moment before looking back at me.

I'd made my decision. "Let's go inside and act natural."

He nodded, but I saw the worry in his eyes. "You sure you want to do this?"

I didn't even have to think about it. Even though my father and I had a strained relationship, I didn't want to see any harm come to him.

With a nod, I inserted my key into the door and stepped inside.

When I spotted Julie and my father sitting at the table, I didn't even have to feign my surprise. Something about seeing the two of them having dinner was intrinsically shocking.

Julie grinned as she raised a glass of wine to her lips. "Camryn. What a surprise to see you here."

I paused near them, trying to keep myself in check. "A surprise? This is my apartment."

Julie giggled and took another sip. "Of course. It was so nice of you to offer it to your father for our dinner since the AC went out in Lavern's place."

Her apartment hadn't felt hot to me, but I didn't say anything. Instead, my gaze went to my father. "Dad."

He nodded back at me, his neck appearing stiff. "Camryn."

Then I looked at the food on his plate.

Fried chicken.

I sucked in a breath.

"It's my special recipe." Julie picked up a bowl loaded with drumsticks and pushed it toward me. "Would you like a piece?"

A sickly feeling trickled in my stomach. "No, thank you."

My dad lifted his piece and began to take a bite. "It's delicious."

Before it reached his lips, I smacked it out of his hands.

"Camryn . . . what's gotten into you?" He stared at me in horror.

"Don't eat that, Dad." I stared at the drumstick on the floor almost as if it might attack, even though I knew that was absurd. "Have you already eaten any?"

"Just a little." His eyebrows shoved together as he stared at me. "Why wouldn't I?"

"Because it's been poisoned." Weston stepped beside me, his muscles bristled.

My father's eyebrows shot up. "Poisoned? Have you lost your mind? Are you so upset with me that you'd go to these extremes?"

Julie sat at the table with an innocent, almost placid expression across her face. "I don't know what's going on here, but maybe I should go. I feel like I'm in the middle of something."

"I think you should stay." Weston stepped closer, his arms crossed over his broad chest as if he were daring her to leave.

Julie stood and placed her napkin on the table. She looked at my father before saying, "I can call you later."

Weston moved in front of her and blocked her exit.

"James . . ." She looked back at my father, an almost timid expression on her face. "I'm beginning to feel uncomfortable."

My dad rose, his gaze stormy now. "What are you two up to? Whatever it is, I don't like it."

"That's rich coming from you," I couldn't help but snap. "We need to call 911. Now."

As I said the words, Julie grabbed my arm and jerked me toward her. Something sharp pricked my skin.

A knife.

Where had that come from?

It didn't matter. Because she held it at my throat.

It took me a moment to process what was happening.

But there was only one thing I was certain about.

Julie had all the capabilities and lack of conscience to kill me . . . while my dad and Weston watched.

"Julie . . ." My dad gasped as his eyes widened and darted back and forth between mine and the woman he'd been pining over.

"You were going to scam me," Julie growled. "I hate when people take advantage of other people. My husband . . . that's what he always did."

"Julie . . . let's talk through this." Dad stepped closer, something close to panic in his usually perfectly composed demeanor.

"Stay back!" Julie barked. "I'll do it. Don't test me. Poisoning is my weapon of choice, but I'm not a one-trick pony. I can use this knife just as effectively."

I felt the blade pricking my skin until I was afraid to breathe. Plus, Julie's erratic motions made me realize that if I made one wrong move, she'd slice the blade across my artery.

I glanced at Weston, and I saw the concern in the lines on his face. He stared at me, and I knew he'd be devastated if something happened to me.

Instantly, my mind went back to the moment we'd been standing beside his truck. To the way I felt his finger brushing up against my cheek. To the way I'd felt when he quietly sang in my ear.

I wanted that again.

Except I wanted more.

With everything on the line, my desires had become so much clearer.

"I'm the one you're upset with." Dad turned to Julie. "Why don't you take this out on me and not Camryn?"

"You were going to try to take my money, weren't you?" Julie's voice sounded clipped and tight. "I can't let you do that. I can't stand the fact you thought I was one of those dumb women who'd fall for your act."

"I never thought you were dumb," he said.

"Oh, let me guess. You like to go for the smart ones because they're more of a challenge." I could practically hear Julie's eyes rolling even though I couldn't see her face. "Give me a break."

"Why did you try to kill Annie?" I asked quietly, trying not to make any unnecessary actions.

I knew Garrison was on the way. I just needed to buy some time until he got here.

Then again, I wasn't sure the detective had a better chance talking Julie into putting down this knife than Weston and my father did.

"I want more for my daughter," Julie said. "I thought if Annie was out of the picture that Lavern would move on to other more prosperous ventures. Maybe she could become a doctor like her father was."

"Then you killed Krissy because you knew that Lavern was going to move on to her next?" Again, I said the words softly so my throat wouldn't move any more than necessary. "Were you just going to keep on going down the line killing people until your daughter gave up? Or until she was rotting in jail?"

"That was never supposed to happen." Julie's voice came out as a harsh, desperate whisper.

"Who did you think would be blamed?" I asked.

"I didn't know! But not me. Not Lavern. Random crimes happen all the time. That Celeste girl should have been looked at more. She's a monster."

"Doesn't this seem a little extreme?" Weston raised his hands in front of him as if to not set Julie off.

"Conversations didn't work." Julie's voice hardened. "So, I had to revert to other means. Plus, that whole online video thing was ridiculous. People actually watch other people eat for fun? And these people get paid for it? What is this society coming to? It disgusts me. I had to work hard. Use my intellect. I worked years and years to accomplish what I did. These people? They set up a camera. They eat like pigs. They're treated like royalty by their fans."

"That still isn't a reason for murder," Weston said.

I doubted Julie even heard him. She was lost in her own delusions right now.

"Everyone needs to stop talking," she screeched. "I have a plan. And it doesn't involve this knife. It involves all of you eating this chicken. And you know who's going to look guilty of this murder/suicide? Camryn Paine."

MY BLOOD WENT COLD.

I'd always heard that expression, but I didn't know it could feel so true.

But every ounce of liquid in my body seemed to turn to ice at her words.

I was there when Annie was hurt. I'd seen the food before she ate it. I *could* have tampered with it.

Now this food was tampered with as well, and Julie was right. The whole thing could look like a murder/suicide.

I thought Garrison was smarter than that, but Julie was also smarter than I gave her credit for. I had to buy some time.

I glanced at my father. His eyes were glazing.

He'd ingested some poison.

It was beginning to affect him, wasn't it?

Panic fluttered through me.

"What possible motive would I have to want to kill Weston and my father?" I asked.

"To you, both of these men are simply men who broke your heart. They used you and then dumped you and then came running back. You know they're both going to do it again."

Something about her words caused hot tears to prick my eyes.

How would Julie have known any of that? I wasn't saying her words were all true. But she'd definitely struck a nerve.

My eyes met Weston's, and I saw the remorse in his gaze.

Her words had struck a nerve with him also.

"So, you're going to say I had a mental break?" I said, trying to buy some time. "Is that what you're hoping the police will think?"

"That's right. Because everyone could see just how obsessed you were with this case."

"What possible motive would I have for trying to kill Annie?" I asked.

"I don't know! Maybe the sound of her eating made you go mad. You're so sensitive to these things from what I've heard."

The knife pricked my skin again.

"Did you plan to set me up from the start?" My

mind raced through everything that had happened as I tried to put all the pieces together.

"No, as a matter of fact I didn't. Then I realized how well you fit. I realized you could play right into my plan. Now here we are."

I glanced at my dad and saw he was even paler.

Flashbacks of Annie hit me. Flashbacks of the way her skin turned white, and her motions slowed right before she collapsed.

We didn't have much time.

"Are you the one who sent those threats to Annie?" I continued, praying backup got here in time.

"I did. I hoped that would make her walk away. It didn't. But I didn't send those threats to Desi. My guess is that he heard what was happening to Annie, and he sent those threats himself, hoping he'd get attention from it."

She might have a point.

But Desi had looked genuinely scared. Maybe what happened with Annie really had shaken him up. Maybe that's why he had gone into hiding.

"Nobody is going to believe that story," Weston said. "I've made a lot of mistakes. So has James. But Camryn is stronger than that. No one is going to believe that she went to these extremes."

"Women do desperate things all the time," Julie huffed, her hot breath hitting my neck.

"If you leave prick marks on Camryn's skin, the police will know something else happened." Dad nodded toward me, his breathing heavier now, his eyes even more glazed.

His words seemed to catch Julie by surprise, and she loosened her grip on me ever so slightly.

As she did, I knew this was my opening.

Moving quickly, I swung my elbow into her chest.

She doubled over in pain but quickly righted herself.

But not before Weston charged her. As their bodies collided, the knife cluttered to the floor.

"I've got it, sweet pea." My father lumbered toward the weapon. His fingers closed over the handle, and he tossed it into the living room.

I glanced back at Julie. Weston grabbed her arms and twisted them behind her, restraining her as her teeth gnashed and her nostrils flared.

Just in time, Garrison burst inside my apartment with three officers.

I glanced at my dad in time to see him collapse to the floor.

"We need an ambulance!" I told Garrison. "Now. My father has been poisoned."

I paced the waiting room floor.

Only a few days ago Jinky had been in this very room at this very hospital doing the very same thing as she waited for an update on her niece.

Now I was waiting to see how my father was doing.

Weston stood from the seat where he'd been perched for the past ten minutes. He didn't pace with me, but he looked ready to catch me if I fell.

The paramedics had brought my dad here. He'd been unresponsive.

Just like Annie.

I knew doctors were doing their best to bring him back.

I hated the thought of him passing on and the two of us ending on such a bad note.

I wished I could take back the words I'd said. Then again, I also wished Dad was just a normal father. An honest one. One I could trust.

Either way, I didn't want this.

Someone stepped into the room, and I saw that it was Jinky. She threw her arms around me.

"Oh, sweetie . . . I'm so sorry," she murmured. "I just heard everything. Julie poisoned my Annie?"

"It's hard to believe, isn't it?" I let out a soft sigh,

unable to avoid my introspection at this turn of events. "I know we want to shape our kids' lives. That there's a part of us that wishes we could control their actions and their futures. But not like this. The line between concern and control . . . it's a fine one, isn't it?"

I thought about Scarlett. I thought about my opposition to her going to Europe. Sure, I had safety concerns for her. But I also couldn't treat her like a child.

I couldn't try to dictate every aspect of her life. Making mistakes was how she would learn and grow.

"Kids have to come to a point where we let them fly," Jinky said. "And I'm sure that's terrifying."

She was right.

It was the same for anyone we cared about. We couldn't hold them back. If we tried, was that really love at all?

Jinky slipped an arm around me. "What a nightmare. But maybe this is all behind us now."

"We can only hope."

As she said those words, the doctor stepped into the room. I glanced at Weston, and he moved to the other side of me as we waited for an update.

The doctor's eyes met mine, and I braced myself for whatever she had to say.

"Your father is awake, and he's going to be okay," Dr. Kenna announced. "Give us a few minutes, and you can go see him."

I nearly collapsed with relief at her words.

My dad was going to hang around a while. Maybe we could repair our relationship.

Maybe.

I could hope and pray, at least.

For now, I wanted to see him with my own eyes.

Because we never knew when these moments would be our last.

That meant I had to embrace every second I'd been given . . . in more than one way.

I LEFT my father's room two hours later. It was getting late, and I couldn't stay at the hospital overnight.

Plus, my dad had already conned the nurses into getting him some extra ice cream.

He was going to be just fine, in his own little way, while he was a patient here.

Garrison had stopped by to check on Dad.

He'd told me that the charges against Lavern had been dropped, and Julie had confessed to everything.

The woman had gone from a raging mad lunatic to having a major meltdown. Garrison had even confided that Julie's husband also may have been poisoned. Apparently, the two of them had a lot of problems, and he'd had a significant life insurance policy.

Cops back in Florida were going to look into his death again.

Julie was clearly a very desperate woman.

I didn't think she was behind Annie's extortion. I'd told Garrison he should look into Desi.

Desi knew what kind of money Annie was making. He seemed exactly like the type who might follow her and do something like that. Garrison suspected the same.

Weston offered to drive me home, and I accepted, of course. The only other alternative was walking.

But the two of us still needed to talk. We hadn't finished that conversation we'd started earlier, and I knew we needed to.

Just like Scarlett, I knew I had to give Weston the freedom to make his own choices. If he stayed here at Grand Isle, I wanted it to be because he wanted to. Because he thought staying was the right thing. Not because I asked him to.

We were relatively quiet on the drive back. But he walked me to my door. Garrison had said they'd gotten everything they needed at the scene, and I could stay here this evening.

As we paused in my living room, I tried to push aside thoughts of what happened earlier.

How lives had almost been lost.

I could still feel the prick of the knife against my neck.

I was so glad Julie's plan hadn't worked.

I cleared my throat and glanced up at Weston. Neither of us bothered to sit. We probably had too much energy built up inside us.

I swallowed hard before saying, "I'm so glad you're okay."

"I'm glad *you* are okay." He pulled me into his arms.

"I was nervous there for a minute. I really was, I admit it." Tears pricked my eyes as reality rolled over me in waves.

"Me too," he whispered.

I pulled back enough to make eye contact with Weston.

If there was one thing all of this had taught me, it was to embrace each moment.

It seemed like I'd been dragging my feet an awfully lot lately.

I licked my lips before saying, "I'm sorry I've been so skittish about us. But I've given things a lot of thought, and if you want to go on the road—"

"I'm staying here," he finished.

My breath caught. "What? Why?"

"I already made that mistake once. If we don't learn from our pasts, then what good are those mistakes we made? At least, we can gain wisdom from them, right?"

That was the exact same thing I'd said about Scarlett. Learning from our mistakes was one of the things that made us stronger and better.

I needed to know this was truly what Weston wanted, however. "That tour is a great opportunity for you."

He shrugged. "I'm still going to have the chance to do a few concerts here and there, but I'm not going to go on a full-blown tour. I moved to Savannah to be close to my kids, and that's what I'm going to do. Even if at times it feels like they don't want to hang out with me or want anything to do with me." He let out a fading chuckle. "I'm still going to be in their lives. And I hope they will appreciate it one day."

"They will."

"And then there's you." His hands pressed into my back, drawing me even closer.

My throat tightened. "Me?"

"I really feel like you coming here to Grand Isle was an answer to prayer. I've had so many regrets over the way things ended between us. And I don't want to push you into something that you're not ready for. But you got it right when you said that we're great friends. And I know we could be more. What I'm not sure about is if you're ready."

I remembered the kiss I'd exchanged with Zeke. I remembered how guilty I felt afterwards, like I'd been cheating on my husband. Emotionally, it had been so hard to handle.

Would I feel that way again with any other man I kissed in the future? I didn't know.

But anxiety churned inside me at the thought.

When I remembered how I'd felt when I thought that Weston could be harmed because of me, I couldn't deny I had feelings for this man.

For once in my life, I needed to throw caution to the wind.

Rising on my tiptoes, I pressed my lips into Weston's.

As cliche as it sounded, fireworks exploded inside me. Even better, it was like fireworks mixed with hot chocolate and gooey marshmallows and warm sand beneath my feet.

It was perfection with no guilt involved.

Instead, this moment felt right. It felt like I was coming home.

As we pulled away, I ran my finger across my lips, remembering the familiar feeling of the kiss. Remembering the closeness we had before. Wanting it again.

My heart sped.

Was this really happening?

I wanted it to.

But I couldn't be reckless.

I swallowed hard, my throat feeling as swollen as my lips. "As much as I'd love to just be carefree, I need to take this slow."

A soft grin feathered across Weston's lips. "I'm not going anywhere. I'm here to stay."

He raked his hands through my hair before pulling me close again and holding me in that way that I'd come to love.

I could stay like this forever . . . maybe we were finally getting our second chance.

~~~

Thank you for reading *Tone Death*. If you enjoyed this book, would you please consider leaving a review?

Stay tuned for *Sonata in the Key of Dead*, coming soon!
~~~

USA TODAY BESTSELLING AUTHOR
CHRISTY BARRITT
SONATA
IN THE
KEY OF
DEAD
SCHOOL OF HARD ROCKS
BOOK FOUR

ALSO BY CHRISTY BARRITT:

YOU MIGHT ALSO ENJOY

...

THE SQUEAKY CLEAN MYSTERY
SERIES

On her way to completing a degree in forensic science, Gabby St. Claire drops out of school and starts her own crime-scene cleaning business. When a routine cleaning job uncovers a murder weapon the police overlooked, she realizes that the wrong person is in jail. She also realizes that crime scene cleaning might be the perfect career for utilizing her investigative skills.

Hazardous Duty is now a movie on PureFlix and will soon air on UPtv!

#1 Hazardous Duty

#2 Suspicious Minds

#2.5 It Came Upon a Midnight Crime (novella)

#3 Organized Grime

THE WORST DETECTIVE EVER:

I'm not really a private detective. I just play one on TV.

Joey Darling, better known to the world as Raven Remington, detective extraordinaire, is trying to separate herself from her invincible alter ego. She played the spunky character for five years on the hit TV show *Relentless*, which catapulted her to fame and into the role of Hollywood's sweetheart. When her marriage falls apart, her finances dwindle to nothing, and her father disappears, Joey finds herself on the Outer Banks of North Carolina, trying to piece together her life away from the limelight. But as people continually mistake her for the character she played on TV, she's tasked with solving real life crimes . . . even though she's terrible at it.

#1 Ready to Fumble

#2 Reign of Error

#3 Safety in Blunders

#4 Join the Flub

#5 Blooper Freak

#6 Flaw Abiding Citizen

#7 Gaffe Out Loud

#8 Joke and Dagger

#9 Wreck the Halls

#10 Glitch and Famous

ABOUT THE AUTHOR

USA Today has called Christy Barritt's books "scary, funny, passionate, and quirky."

Christy writes both mystery and romantic suspense novels that are clean with underlying messages of faith. Her books have won the Daphne du Maurier Award for Excellence in Suspense and Mystery, have been twice nominated for the Romantic Times Reviewers' Choice Award, and have finaled for both a Carol Award and Foreword Magazine's Book of the Year.

She is married to her Prince Charming, a man who thinks she's hilarious—but only when she's not trying to be. Christy is a self-proclaimed klutz, an avid music lover who's known for spontaneously bursting into song, and a road trip aficionado.

When she's not working or spending time with her family, she enjoys singing, playing the guitar, and exploring small, unsuspecting towns where people have no idea how accident-prone she is.

Find Christy online at:
   www.christybarritt.com
   www.facebook.com/christybarritt
   www.twitter.com/cbarritt

Sign up for Christy's newsletter to get information on all of her latest releases here: **www.christybarritt. com/newsletter-sign-up/**

COMPLETE BOOK LIST

Squeaky Clean Mysteries:
- #1 Hazardous Duty
- #2 Suspicious Minds
- #2.5 It Came Upon a Midnight Crime (novella)
- #3 Organized Grime
- #4 Dirty Deeds
- #5 The Scum of All Fears
- #6 To Love, Honor and Perish
- #7 Mucky Streak
- #8 Foul Play
- #9 Broom & Gloom
- #10 Dust and Obey
- #11 Thrill Squeaker
- #11.5 Swept Away (novella)
- #12 Cunning Attractions
- #13 Cold Case: Clean Getaway

#14 Cold Case: Clean Sweep

#15 Cold Case: Clean Break

#16 Cleans to an End

While You Were Sweeping, A Riley Thomas Spinoff

The Sierra Files:

#1 Pounced

#2 Hunted

#3 Pranced

#4 Rattled

The Gabby St. Claire Diaries (a Tween Mystery series):

The Curtain Call Caper

The Disappearing Dog Dilemma

The Bungled Bike Burglaries

The Worst Detective Ever

#1 Ready to Fumble

#2 Reign of Error

#3 Safety in Blunders

#4 Join the Flub

#5 Blooper Freak

#6 Flaw Abiding Citizen

#7 Gaffe Out Loud

#8 Joke and Dagger

#9 Wreck the Halls

#10 Glitch and Famous

Raven Remington

Relentless

Holly Anna Paladin Mysteries:

#1 Random Acts of Murder

#2 Random Acts of Deceit

#2.5 Random Acts of Scrooge

#3 Random Acts of Malice

#4 Random Acts of Greed

#5 Random Acts of Fraud

#6 Random Acts of Outrage

#7 Random Acts of Iniquity

Lantern Beach Mysteries

#1 Hidden Currents

#2 Flood Watch

#3 Storm Surge

#4 Dangerous Waters

#5 Perilous Riptide

#6 Deadly Undertow

Lantern Beach Romantic Suspense

Tides of Deception

Shadow of Intrigue

Storm of Doubt
Winds of Danger
Rains of Remorse
Torrents of Fear

Lantern Beach P.D.
On the Lookout
Attempt to Locate
First Degree Murder
Dead on Arrival
Plan of Action

Lantern Beach Escape
Afterglow (a novelette)

Lantern Beach Blackout
Dark Water
Safe Harbor
Ripple Effect
Rising Tide

Lantern Beach Guardians
Hide and Seek
Shock and Awe
Safe and Sound

Lantern Beach Blackout: The New Recruits

Rocco

Axel

Beckett

Gabe

Lantern Beach Mayday

Run Aground

Dead Reckoning

Tipping Point

Lantern Beach Blackout: Danger Rising

Brandon

Dylan

Maddox

Titus

Lantern Beach Christmas

Silent Night

Crime á la Mode

Dead Man's Float

Milkshake Up

Bomb Pop Threat

Banana Split Personalities

Vanishing Ranch

Forgotten Secrets

Necessary Risk (coming soon)

The Sidekick's Survival Guide
The Art of Eavesdropping
The Perks of Meddling
The Exercise of Interfering
The Practice of Prying
The Skill of Snooping
The Craft of Being Covert

Saltwater Cowboys
Saltwater Cowboy
Breakwater Protector
Cape Corral Keeper
Seagrass Secrets
Driftwood Danger
Unwavering Security

Beach House Mysteries
The Cottage on Ghost Lane
The Inn on Hanging Hill
The House on Dagger Point

School of Hard Rocks Mysteries
The Treble with Murder
Crime Strikes a Chord
Tone Death

Carolina Moon Series

Home Before Dark

Gone By Dark

Wait Until Dark

Light the Dark

Taken By Dark

Suburban Sleuth Mysteries:

Death of the Couch Potato's Wife

Fog Lake Suspense:

Edge of Peril

Margin of Error

Brink of Danger

Line of Duty

Legacy of Lies

Secrets of Shame

Refuge of Redemption

Cape Thomas Series:

Dubiosity

Disillusioned

Distorted

Standalone Romantic Mystery:

The Good Girl

Suspense:

Imperfect

The Wrecking

Sweet Christmas Novella:

Home to Chestnut Grove

Standalone Romantic-Suspense:

Keeping Guard

The Last Target

Race Against Time

Ricochet

Key Witness

Lifeline

High-Stakes Holiday Reunion

Desperate Measures

Hidden Agenda

Mountain Hideaway

Dark Harbor

Shadow of Suspicion

The Baby Assignment

The Cradle Conspiracy

Trained to Defend

Mountain Survival

Dangerous Mountain Rescue

Nonfiction:

Characters in the Kitchen

Changed: True Stories of Finding God through Christian Music (out of print)

The Novel in Me: The Beginner's Guide to Writing and Publishing a Novel (out of print)